CLOSE TO THE SUN AGAIN

Close to the Sun Again

A NEW NOVEL BY

MORLEY CALLAGHAN

MACMILLAN OF CANADA / TORONTO

Canadian Cataloguing in Publication Data

Callaghan, Morley, 1903-
   Close to the sun again

ISBN 0-7705-1574-6

I. Title.

PS8505.A41C56   C813'.5'2   C77-001310-4
PR9199.3.C343C56

The Macmillan Company of Canada Limited
70 Bond Street, Toronto M5B 1X3

CLOSE TO THE SUN AGAIN

ONE

Wherever he went in the world, and he had been in all his great corporation's outposts, Ira Groome was soon called "The Commander". Not that he ever mentioned his former naval rank, or his great record in the North Atlantic. People simply felt more comfortable with him and themselves calling him Commander, for in spite of thirty years in civilian life, he still carried with him all the war marks of a superior officer; just as he carried the old seaman Horler with him as his man; just as he carried his elegant old Rolls-Royce with him wherever he went. Tall and straight-backed, he still had that relaxed assurance of the naval man. He kept his voice down as if he were still on a ship's bridge at the voice tube giving steering instructions. And just as a captain on a ship can't afford to get personally involved with any member of his crew and has to be utterly impersonal, he had no personal involvements with anyone who worked for him. This meant that he could be utterly ruthless with his underlings, and yet fair, because he had no close personal relationships with any of them. He was good-humored and at ease with men in locker rooms. Rich men loved having him around. In his company they felt less threatened.

It was as if Ira Groome had never left the service. He had merely found another admiral in some far-off head office whose signals he obeyed with discipline and distinction. It was, too, as if he had forgotten, long ago forgotten, that before the war he had been another kind of a man with another kind of nature, a young man full of curiosity about people, an archeology student who had been on digs in the Yucatan. But in his way of life now, he was this other man, this Commander who might never again be able to hear the voices in his own heart.

In his seventh year in São Paulo, where his Brazilian Power Corporation had a three-billion-dollar investment in public utilities, little things began to happen that he found hard to cope with. As the company's Lord in São Paulo he had enormous political influence. He lived in high style with his wife, Julia, whom he had met at college and married at the war's end. He had a son, Chris, a college drop-out, who was in the United States. Ira Groome played tennis well, rode horses, and entertained lavishly. He was a charming host, but was often left alone to do the job, for Julia was an alcoholic. She had given him a lot of trouble, but he had put up with her with a grace and concern that was much admired. Colonels courted him, and saw to it that beautiful young women were in his company. Otherwise he would have been alone at night, for his wife was in a São Paulo nursing home with her liver rotting away.

In the morning of the day Julia died Ira Groome was at her bedside, watching her come out of a heavy sleep. Then her eyes finally opening were on him, the eyes clouded as if she were still in a dream, and these eyes in that puffed and ruined face were suddenly filled with wonder as she came out of the dream and saw him there. "Ira, Ira," she whispered, as if he was really there for her now, as he had been at another time years ago before they had married, when she had belonged in his easy-going life. As she held him now with her wondering, eager eyes it was as if she was living, in that one bare dreaming moment, all the life she had missed with him. "It's you, Ira," she whispered. "Ah, it's really you."

"It's me all right, Julia," he said, upset by her frail eagerness. "I'm here."

But at the sound of his voice her mind cleared, and as she stared at him and placed him, the wonder went out of her eyes and all the expectancy, too, and she turned her head away. "No," she whispered. Then he could hardly hear the broken words coming from the pillow. She had comprehended that the Ira Groome who had been in her mind, enchanting her in a dreamed-of life, was not the one who was beside her now. "Why were you such a stranger to me . . . after you married me?" she whispered. "Where did you go, Ira? Was there someone else? Someone you couldn't forget?"

"That's absurd," he said gently, but he couldn't go on. He was too surprised and hurt. Everyone knew how kind he had been to her. Everyone had told him he had been heroic in his patient acceptance of her condition. She said no more. She fell asleep. And while he sat beside her nursing his painful surprise, and knowing that she was dying, he wondered what it was she had missed in him. He sat there motionless for a long time. Then he wondered what it was that he had missed in himself, and then it was like a sudden awareness of the loss of a limb, and like feeling the pain of it for the first time. Then, as he stood up and hesitantly brushed Julia's hair from her forehead, he wondered why he had the strange feeling that life would go on passing him by until . . . until what . . . until when?

When Julia died he waited uneasily for his son to come from the States for the funeral. Chris, who now was as tall as his father, but very thin and gangling, had long hair and played a guitar. He had written few letters, none to his father, just a few to his mother. In the car after the funeral Ira Groome wanted to draw Chris closer to him, and talk out of that painful astonishment he felt about Julia, but he couldn't break through his own stoic manner. "Now we'll do the best we can. Bear up, eh, Chris? Bear up," which wasn't what he wanted to say at all. It wasn't the voice he thought was in his heart. "Yeah, terrific," Chris

3

said. When they had got out of the car at the hotel, with Horler waiting for instructions, Chris said, "Well, sir, now that's over, don't expect to hear from me again," and he walked away. He left town that night.

The next day in his office Ira Groome did an odd thing. His secretary, Miss McCandless, an English girl from the London office who had wanted to be transferred to São Paulo because she could speak Portuguese, had got deeply involved with an army officer. When she came to work in the morning her eyes would be tired and red-rimmed as if she had cried all night long. That morning Ira Groome, noting her eyes for the first time, had flowers put on her desk. Later in the day she came into his huge office with the great windows. "Thank you for the flowers, Commander." She sounded ill at ease and apprehensive.

"It's all right, Miss McCandless," he said, holding her with his silence. "Look, is there anything I can do?" he said. Aghast that he could be aware of her trouble she said quickly, "No, sir," and fled. He wanted to say, "Wait, you're missing something. I'm not an unfeeling man." Then suddenly he wondered if he hadn't used these words because he knew he was the one who was missing something. That girl couldn't believe he might now feel close to her. Nor could Chris. Nor could he himself. All his habits, his style, were confining him so tightly now, and he was trying to break out.

Then two days later, when three visiting directors came to talk with him about government proposals to nationalize the great utilities company, and he had been in the boardroom with them all afternoon, another little thing happened. He had begun to listen to them with a detachment unworthy of him.

Everything had been said, everything considered, everyone seen who had to be seen, and he had said, "I can assure you, gentlemen, that we'll be harassed for three or four months. But they simply haven't got the money, and they don't trust the companies who want to come in on it. We'll have to put up with some expensive bribing, then we'll be left alone for a few more years." The three visiting directors, Henry Gordon, Albert Rogers, and Jay Windspeare, were all in their fifties, all with good crops of hair, all with deprecating smiles. Only one of them, Rogers, was given to talking in obscenities. Gordon, in fact, was a bit of a scholar. Expressing confidence in Groome's judgment, they began to joke with each other while he, detached now, looked out the window. Then into his mind came a picture of crowded São Paulo streets under neon lights; gleaming brown faces, brightly dressed women, black faces, pimps, pickpockets, entrepreneurs, the street always a bazaar where strange, unpredictable, exciting things could happen; and then, turning, he looked at his colleagues. Gordon was shifting uncomfortably on his chair; he had hemorrhoids; Rogers had just taken a glass of water with a tablet for his ulcer. As he looked at them, Ira Groome felt that pain and astonishment that had been growing in him since his dying wife had shocked him. These weren't his people, he thought. These careful men, these bookkeepers who knew only the tragedies of trivia, and nothing of a beauty born in excess. Then who were his people? Where were his people? And carried along in a daydream that was so strange for him he thought of lawless men and women, holed up somewhere, nursing passions that made life so real.

Letting himself be carried on he reached for those wild faces he couldn't make out; he reached for the excitement, the intensity of their ruthless passions and their suffering; he couldn't feel it. He felt fettered, pushed away, scorned, and doomed to stay where he was and as he was. Yet why? What had he done? Where had he done it? When? If he could only relive scenes in his life, open the bank of his unused memory. Relive. If he could get to the right place before it was too late — then life could not go on passing him by . . .

Just in time he caught himself and caught, too, the silence in the room and the sympathy in his colleagues' eyes; their eyes were saying openly that they knew he was saddened by his wife, and he squirmed in embarrassment. I'm too old for this kind of nonsense. No more of it. Never again, he thought grimly. And right there, as they all stood up talking about getting together for dinner, he told himself that the simple truth must be that he was bored now with his life in São Paulo. He had had it.

Two weeks later he notified the head office he was handing in his resignation. When they pleaded with him to stay on, he laughed and wouldn't budge. They offered him the post in Madrid. He had liked Spain. They offered him the Tokyo post. He told them he was going home, a good place to make up his mind what he wanted to do. Before he left São Paulo there were many

5

long-distance phone calls from the head office and from civic leaders, friends of the head office bent on keeping him in harness, all appealing to his sense of service and stressing the community's need of a man like him. They talked to him about their police commission. A strong man was needed as chairman. The day before he got home a picture and story appeared in the local newspapers. Commander Groome, the Brazilian Power Company's Lord in São Paulo had agreed to be the police commission's chairman. He would be taking over the fine old Wilkinson place on the ravine as soon as it was made ready.

He came in by plane with Horler on a night unseasonably hot for the end of September, and by ten they were in the taxi on the road along the lakeshore, and soon they could see against the sky in the misty heat the city's towers in rising floors of light. He had no close friends in this city. Those he knew well belonged in the corporate world established in those rising layers of light with floodlit crowns. The new city. It was getting newer every day. A gleaming red ball of light was atop the tallest tower in the world. And far below was the hotel which had once been so high and dominating, now just another big lighted block.

In the lobby three people had been awaiting his arrival. Tom McNally, the assistant manager, had come out of his office to check on arrivals from the airport. A dapper, ageless man, he had been with the hotel for twenty years. Guests who hadn't been in the hotel for years and yet remembered McNally would stare at his black hair and believe it was dyed. It wasn't. McNally also had a wife his age who looked as young as he did. This afternoon McNally had got a phone call from Angus McMurtry, a blunt and ruthless man, whose bank held the mortgage on the hotel, telling him to look after Commander Groome. "Let me know when Commander Groome comes in," he said to the clerk at the registration desk and went back to his office.

Eva Meadows, who now stood over by the elevators, was a simply and elegantly dressed woman in her late thirties with golden-brown hair and a striking warm and mellow beauty which seemed to be put out of reach of everyone by her manner of repose and contemplation. She had just come from the bar, where she had dismissed her brash escort. Here by the elevators she could watch the desk while pretending to glance impatiently at her wrist watch. An educated, expensive, and very discriminating hooker, she had read about Ira Groome; she made it her business to keep track of rich and single businessmen coming to the hotel.

The third one, now far down the lobby near the eastern entrance, had spoken to NcNally. He was a prematurely white-haired man with a funny tweed hat and an expensive camel-hair jacket. Leo Cawthra was the popular columnist of the *World*. He held court in this lobby where middle-aged women and gray-haired men, passing him, liked to call out eagerly, "Good evening Mr. Cawthra," hoping he would acknowledge the greeting, which he always did with a graceful gesture. Years ago Leo Cawthra had been a close, warm friend of Ira Groome's. They had been young naval lieutenants together. But Leo Cawthra had come to believe that Ira Groome stood for everything he himself hated. Over the years, calling himself an Ira Groome watcher, he had waited to hear that the Commander had driven someone crazy or had gone crazy himself. A lot of time had passed, there had been other wars, and now that Leo Cawthra had found out what had happened in Ira Groome's personal life he wanted to do a column on him. As he saw it, a man of Ira Groome's stature shouldn't be coming home and bothering to head up a local police commission. Leo Cawthra couldn't imagine "Ribbons" Groome sitting around in the police building with cops in every corridor, defining police policy and allotting funds with the likes of old Judge Benton, the moralist, and the rich psychiatrist Dr. Honnsburger, who had got himself appointed for some cunning reason of his own, and the third one, smiling Mayor Stronack. Unless it was that Ira Groome had come to a point in his life where there was nothing else left for him. Unless he had indeed gone a little crazy.

And Leo Cawthra, while taking little bows from faithful readers who passed by, kept his eye on the desk where those who had come from the airport were now lining up to register. The first ones were all middle-aged; men in wrinkled, loose, light summer suits, their faces sweaty from the heat, their ties pulled away from their shirt collars, and women who pulled at the necklines of their dresses. And then came eight pretty young girls all in a row, coming magically out of nowhere, all cool, happy-faced and smiling.

Ira Groome and Horler, who had come in, were not in the

line at the desk. Thirty feet away across a wide oriental rug Ira Groome took up his position behind four expensive pigskin bags, a little fortress wall between him and those lining up. A porter stood to one side, watching the bags. Horler, stout, gray, and heavy, was the one who approached the desk to look after the registration. He didn't get in the line-up.

"Commander Groome," he said to a busy clerk who looked, blinked, then called McNally, who quickly appeared to look after the registration himself.

"A good flight, I hope, Mr. Horler," McNally said.

"Not bad at all. Hot here, isn't it?"

"The last rose of summer."

"That's pretty good. The last rose of summer. Yeah!"

"You'll have an adjoining room in the suite, Mr. Horler."

"I'm sure it will be all right."

"If the Commander is not too tired he can catch the last show in The Room."

"I'll mention it to him."

"Just phone down. There'll be a table for him."

McNally hardly glanced at the Commander, whom he had eyed when he came out of the office. He had arranged to have the biggest basket of fruit on the table in the Commander's suite, and a box of chocolate mints. Few guests on arrival got the chocolate mints. The fruit, yes, but not the mints too. McNally had been informed that Commander Groome was rich, and all the corporation men in town would be aware he was at the hotel. And Cawthra would be doing a column on him.

From her post near the elevators Eva Meadows, spotting Ira Groome and recognizing him from his picture, came toward him slowly with her detached and superior air as if there was something else on her mind. Miss Meadows had never had a pimp because it had never been necessary for her to solicit anyone; just to be seen, just to stop and meditate and let a man's eyes take in her fine mellow elegance was enough. She had liked what she had read about Ira Groome. A rich man with influence. A single man of fifty-three, a most vulnerable age. A man who had been a great war hero. A man who had won so many naval decorations on the North Atlantic he had been called "Ribbons" Groome. And in a grand march through the corporations he seemed to have got all the ribbons there, too.

Rich ribbons! Just her style. And she crossed the wide rug in her slow steps, then stopped suddenly with her faint, wise smile. "Commander Groome, I believe?"

"That's right."

"Well, Eva is my name . . . "

Appraising her for a moment, then getting the hang of her exactly, he said, "See Horler, my dear."

"Horler?"

"Over there at the desk."

"Who's Horler?"

"Horler'll look into it for you."

"Horler . . . " she said uncertainly, and then, "To hell with Horler," yet she managed to smile as if she had just greeted an old friend, and crossing the rug on the way back to the elevators she passed Cawthra who was heading for the desk.

Since Cawthra had the advantage of knowing what had happened in Ira Groome's personal life he was now enchanted with the wisdom of his own youth. He could afford now to be sympathetic, even moved a little, because they had been young together. Why had Groome cleared out of São Paulo? To come here? To take a humpty-dumpty police commission job? To shut himself off in the Wilkinson place with the high brick wall around it? Yesterday Cawthra had asked the financial editor if he could find out in circles here in town what had happened to Ira Groome's wife, Julia, whom Cawthra remembered as a bright and lovely girl. Just two hours ago the financial editor told him what he had found out by way of gossip from the Brazilian Power office. After the war Julia Groome hadn't been able to get used to Ira. She had called him "The Commander" till the day she died. His son, too, had always referred to him as "The Commander". In the march through the corporations Julia had given Ira Groome a bad time; she had become a drunk, and when he had important people in his house she would appear suddenly and put on clowning acts. His sympathetic associates told him she was crazy and he should have put her away long ago. But he carried himself with great dignity. No matter what she did, he treated her with an almost formal courtesy. She liked to travel by herself. She was always going off to some other country, always by plane. And he would be at the airport when she returned, waiting with a wheel chair, for on long flights she got very drunk and had to be carried off the plane to the chair.

9

After she died, Ira Groome had a quarrel with his son Chris, who behaved outrageously. Chris had been given a splendid sense of discipline; he could have been a great officer. But suddenly he dropped out of college, throwing away everything that had held his life together, and told his father he didn't want to see him again. Now, he was off somewhere in Africa, with long hair and a guitar and his bag of marijuana. And Cawthra, having been given these facts about Ira Groome, said softly, "The poor son of a bitch. It took a long time, but life caught up with him." Yet now that these things which ought to have happened to Ira Groome had happened, Cawthra could afford to be sentimental. He wanted to talk to Ira Groome and say, *"What was it that made you change? What happened to you way back there, Ira?"* Then he heard the voice calling, "Horler." The raised voice, coming from a distance, caused everyone to turn, yet the tone implied that it did not matter whether they turned. And there was Horler, now plump, heavy-faced, gray-haired, Horler who had been the bosun on the corvette. Standing only a few feet from Cawthra, he called, "Yes, Commander."

"Don't forget the cigars, Horler."

"Okay, sir."

Cawthra, following Horler's eyes thirty feet across the rug to Ira Groome behind his little fortress of pigskin bags, went toward him, expecting to be recognized. Then he hesitated, losing his confidence, for Ira Groome was still a tall, handsome, lean-faced man in his expensive dark suit and black Irish linen hat. Even the bellhop, who had called another bellhop to help him with the luggage, was keeping his distance, and eyeing Ira Groome's black shoes — bench-made alligator leather from London. And the London-tailored five-hundred-dollar pin-striped suit was so neatly fitted it made the suits of other men near the desk look loose and baggy. Although he had just got off the plane the collar of his champagne-colored shirt was unwrinkled. The sense of authority he exuded standing there alone was even more impressive than it had been at the height of his naval days. His poor wife Julia? His son? No marks on Ira Groome at all. He was the same man, and looked very much the same, too. Just a little heavier. And when he took off his linen hat to touch his forehead with the handerkerchief he removed from his sleeve, his hair looked as thick as ever with just some streaks of gray at the temples; it was still combed straight back. Only his eyes had changed. In the old days, when off by himself like this, his eyes would be grim with hard determination. Now the eyes had something new in them. A fierce, eager reaching, or a restlessness, an expression that actually made him look younger, Cawthra thought, in surprise.

Then the second bellhop came with the room keys, and the two of them, picking up the bags, remained ten feet behind while Ira Groome marched grandly to the elevator's open door. Other guests who had stepped in were waiting. Just as Ira Groome was about to enter, he called. "Horler. Here we are," in the same raised voice, as if there was no one else in the lobby or in the elevator, and he made them wait while Horler came hurrying with the cigars. Still holding them up, Ira Groome gave instructions to one of the bellhops about carrying a particular piece of luggage. He got Horler and the bags into the elevator. Two passengers, with mystified and slightly stunned expressions, found themselves stepping out to make room and to wait for the next elevator. "Thank you. Thank you," Ira Groome said, without looking at them, and the elevator door closed.

McNally, watching from the desk, grinned, reflected, then nodded in serious admiration.

Miss Meadows, still glancing at her wrist watch, had headed for the elevator as if she had made up her mind, and there she stood watching the hand on the elevator clock. The hand stopped at the seventh floor. Horler on the seventh floor! She now understood Horler's role.

Cawthra, who had followed, still believing he might be recognized, had stopped suddenly. When the elevator door closed he turned away, then stopped again as it came to him with a certainty that stunned him that even if he had appeared there in his naval uniform, looking as he had looked twenty-five years ago when they had been such good close friends, Ira Groome still would not have remembered him.

11

TWO ~~~~~~~~~~~~~~~~~~~~~~~~~~~~~~~~~~~~~~

The old Wilkinson place on the ravine, with its wide lawns, great elms, its garden and swimming pool, was enclosed by a brick wall with two iron gates; the big high one at the entrance to the front drive, and the smaller one, a garden gate. Here Horler, doubling as houseman and chauffeur, was on hand for all the little personal services. No matter what Horler did around the house he never lost his air of deference. When talking to Ira Groome directly, or referring to him in a conversation with a neighbor, he was always "The Commander". But now for the first time in years, Horler was not sure about the Commander's plans. It seemed to him that they weren't settling into the place.

The lovely old house with the great Georgian staircase seemed to be just a place to live in for a while. And the Commander wasn't sleeping well. Horler would wake up and hear him in the room below, moving around in the middle of the night, the step so deliberate he was sure the Commander was making a careful plan. Soon he would hear that they were going somewhere else. Maybe the Commander already knew where. Horler couldn't understand this. The Commander shouldn't conceal his plans from him. He had once said, simply and gruffly, "You know, Commander, when the time comes for you to die, I have a feeling I'll die shortly afterwards."

Late at night when the Commander couldn't sleep he would call Horler, and they would sit in the library, keeping each other company, have a few drinks and play cribbage, gin rummy, or chess. He had taught Horler to play chess. When Horler's own wife had died he had been lonely, but only for a short time. He had found that in doing many of the things she had done for the Commander, he had been comforted.

Around the house Horler wore a white jacket. In the car he wore a blue cap and a blue Norfolk jacket. The car, an elegantly preserved ten-year-old Phantom Rolls-Royce, had been shipped from São Paulo. Whenever Ira Groome came out the front door he was a noticeably expensive and distinguished figure, especially if the old war wound in his leg bothered him and he leaned on his cane while Horler opened the car door. After a ceremonial bow Horler would get in behind the wheel and they would half-circle the drive and roll out through the big iron gate for a long drive around the city. Horler believed the Commander was getting to know his way around the new domain. And by the end of the first week Miss Meadows had been called to the house. She had seen Horler, who had made the arrangements.

She came in the middle of the afternoon, stayed for an hour, then sauntered down the drive to meet a taxi at the gate. In those sunlit days she was a full-breasted woman with golden hair that had a tint of red in it, and in the still-warm late afternoon autumn light, walking lazily in all her pretty ripeness, she belonged to the golden glint on the falling brown and red leaves and drifting streams of smoke from the garden next door where raked-up leaves were burning. She came again and again till Horler, who was a great gossip himself, reported that neighbors were talking about Miss Meadows. For a while then she left by the side gate. But by this time the corporation people had put out the word to influential businessmen of social prominence that Ira Groome was to be looked after. Invitations came to sit in boxes at the race track and at the theater. Merchants and their wives got in touch with him and invited him to their dinner parties. The Hunt Club crowd took him up, and came to the house.

Now, in the evenings, taking advantage of the unseasonable warm weather, they sat around the swimming pool, so green in the floodlight, with the moon shining through the tall elm trees, and Horler was there with his movable bar. In the room across the terrace was a long table heaped with cold cuts and pastries. No young people came to the house till Mrs. Oscar Finley arrived with some of the Hunt Club crowd. She wasn't really young; yet at thirty-nine, she could have passed for twenty-five with her kind of figure, black hair, and blue eyes. She was a Porter. The Porters, leather-goods people of the Porter farm, were an old riding and hunting family. Carol Finley had thirty horses of her own at her stables, hunters and hackneys, and she had always been as much at ease with delivery boys as she was with trust company presidents. With his splendid, impersonal, almost mechanical courtesy, Ira Groome was at ease with her. He was at the pool-side table one night with Angus McMurtry, the bank president, and Tom Mathews of the local Brazilian Power office. He had one hand on McMurtry's chair and one on Mathews', and he was wearing a double-breasted white flannel jacket. Mathews said to McMurtry, "I'm going to miss Ira. He's a great man to have beside you in a boardroom, makes you feel invulnerable," and he looked up and smiled at Ira Groome.

"Well, at least you're here with us, Commander," McMurtry said, "and I feel better that you're here." McMurtry, a craggy-faced, humorless man of sixty with a stomach ulcer and a worried wife, was having trouble with his own board of directors. His whole life had been the banking business. He had no formal education and had no small talk and he envied Tom Mathews his ease and his good looks, and the fact that he had more money of his own than he had, and could have a cultural figure like Dr. Morton Hyland to dinner. In the last six months all these little things had begun to make McMurtry feel insecure.

14

When Tom Mathews began talking about the enquiry into police brutality that was going on, McMurtry kept glancing up at Ira Groome. There he was in his white jacket. In his presence a man could feel a little more protected in his own life. "Excuse me," Ira Groome said suddenly. He had seen Mrs. Finley all by herself on the lawn at the end of the pool looking up at a treetop.

"What's up there in the tree?" he asked when he had joined her. "A cat?"

"No. Something just struck me, Commander."

"Well ... "

"What would you say if a thousand many-colored festive balloons suddenly came floating down and we all jumped up and started doing a snake dance around the pool?"

"I'd be surprised," he said, and after a pause he added stiffly, "If we're all so heavy, sedate, and dull, why do you come here, Mrs. Finley?"

"Horses," she said.

"I'm the one who doesn't own a horse."

"Petunias then."

"Petunias?"

"Yes, I've been taking a look at your garden. No petunias. I have no petunias in my garden, either. I can't stand people who go in for petunias, so you see we have something in common. By the way, why does Angus McMurtry keep eyeing you?"

"When was this?"

"I must be showing my ... well ... "

"Hmm," he said. "Don't let me provoke you."

"Why not?"

"Well, why not? Yes, why not stay around?"

She stayed around after the others had left. He led her up to the bedroom. Nothing was said. He took her with a good-humored, workmanlike lack of sentimental nonsense. "You were really very good, my dear," he said. And she, mocking his stiffness, said in a gruff military tone, "Well, sir, seems to me you knew what you were up to."

Sitting around for a nightcap she tried to get close to him, talking about herself. At first she was stunned when he kept calling her "my dear", and then this stiff manner of his began to interest and even move her. She was a very candid woman. She told him all about her family and her marriage. She told him

15

that what she did not know about him was more interesting than what she did know about her husband.

She had married Oscar Finley, a young Olympic horseman. All her friends had admired Oscar's riding and his boyishness at the fairs, she said. But he couldn't always be on a horse, nor could she. She had been the dressage champion at the club. She had expected obedience and tractability in a horse, but not so much of it in a husband. It soon became apparent that he was more comfortable with her horses than he was with her. Last year, making an effort to save the marriage, she had taken Oscar on an expensive African safari. But even in the jungle at night, hearing the roar of a lion or the cry of a jackal, they couldn't huddle together in silence. They had felt further apart and lonelier than they had been back home.

"In a jungle. Trying to get close to a man. Hmm! Interesting," he said. "Hmm." The wild jungle stuff had quickened his curiosity about her strange eyes. She had blue eyes that never lit up, not suddenly, anyway, but were always bright. But the brightness had a misty quality that gave them a glazed, dreamy expression, as if she were high on cocaine, and yet he was sure she never took drugs.

"Your eyes . . . you have rather crazy eyes, Carol," he said.

"So have you," she said.

"Me?"

"Very lonely eyes."

"No one else ever said so."

"Anyway, you're the one who's crazy," she said. "Why do you keep looking at me as if you expect to be reminded suddenly of something or someone? What is it?"

"I really don't know," he said after musing awhile. "I really don't. And I've always had such a good memory." For a moment he remained off by himself, perplexed and wondering, then he saw that she was glad she could bother him, and he laughed.

This was two nights before the press reception at the City Hall. After the reception his picture was in the newspaper. It was a large picture of him and Mayor Stronack at the reception where drinks and sandwiches had been served to the press and members of the city council. The Mayor, who was one of the commissioners, wore a suit that looked conspicuously new on him when he stood beside the immaculate Ira Groome. The cut

16

lines under the picture told a little story. The reporter asked the new Chairman, "You've lived in a certain style, Commander. Do you think that a citizen making a complaint about police brutality will be willing to believe you can listen with the feelings of an ordinary man?" And Ira Groome, with the amused, disdainful smile he wore in the picture, said, "I never had any respect for men of influence and importance who like to pretend in the way they look and act that they are ordinary men."

THREE

Horler brought him to the Commission meetings in the police building where he opened the door of the Rolls-Royce with his ceremonial bow, and was always there waiting for him after a meeting. The second time Horler came to pick him up, he asked Horler to wait a minute while he took a little stroll through the neighborhood. His father, the doctor, used to walk along these streets; he had often walked them himself. He didn't go far away from the car. The neighborhood had changed too much; it didn't look like anything that had ever belonged to him. Houses were unpainted, trees were bare, dead leaves were heaped along the curb, and he returned to the car, put his hands on his hips, and said to Horler, "Ever talk to yourself, Horler?"

18

"Sure, everybody does. Why, sir?"

"I just heard myself say, 'Not here.' "

"Not here?"

"That's right. Not here."

"What's that supposed to mean, sir?"

"I don't know, Horler."

"Not here. Well, then, where?"

"Exactly, Horler," he said, shrugging and smiling as he got into the car.

Just as he couldn't adjust to this neighborhood where the old mansions of his father's time were broken up into apartments and gray rooming houses, his colleagues on the Commission had difficulty in adjusting to his mannerisms. The Police Chief, a tough, stubborn old cop named Bolton, had expected to go on having the Commission eat out of his hand. With Ira Groome at the head of the table, the Chief showed he wasn't sure of himself. He gave stiff and grudging explanations of routine matters and acted as if he believed Ira Groome looked down on him. Nor were complaining citizens or young cops defending themselves ever at ease. Ira Groome, majestic at the head of the table, would cut in with a "Sir . . . ", his head going back imperiously. This "Sir . . . " might mean, "I didn't hear you. Say it again." Or it could mean, "Do you really believe what you are saying, and am I expected to believe it?" Or "Sir" could be so challenging that the man would have to stop in his statement and look ashamed. In no time Ira Groome was in charge of things, and in charge of his colleagues, too. Having made himself thoroughly familiar with the police act and the areas of his authority, he had also made himself familiar with the vanities of the old Judge, the Mayor, and the smiling psychiatrist. It was as if he had been briefed on them. He continually appealed to the Judge as "a man of conscience", and the Judge, bemused and flattered, showed that he believed Ira Groome had recognized him as the Commission's spiritual force. Ira Groome had found out from one of the secretaries, whom he had taken to lunch, that the Judge had led a difficult life with his wife; for the last two years he hadn't spoken a word to her. He wrote notes to her even at dinnertime. On weekends the Judge got a little drunk and at midnight visited an old priest at the Cathedral, who talked and drank with him till he was able to see all things again in a spiritual light. Soon the Judge was saying of Ira Groome, "I divide men into two classes. Those who have weight, and those who have no weight. I say the Commander has weight. We're fortunate to have him."

The smiling Mayor was even easier to handle. He had strong labor support, but businessmen regarded him dubiously. They even patronized him. Ira Groome took him to a Hunt Club party at Mrs. Finley's place. He had him to lunch with some of the big Brazilian Power people. They talked to him about a man of his popular appeal widening his political horizons, and from then on he cultivated Ira Groome and became his man.

As for the psychiatrist, Dr. Honnsburger, Ira Groome wasted little time on him and his cherished sense of intellectual superiority. He said that Honnsburger had "the ingratiating smile of a false priest", and when Honnsburger heard of this remark he felt insecure, was afraid to smile in Ira Groome's presence, and always took care to refer to him as the Commander.

Driving himself along, Ira Groome acted as if he was sure that here in town he was where he wanted to be. He did more than was expected of him. He even did things he shouldn't have done. Yet who was there to tell him to stop? Appearing in the corridors of the police building and saying "Good morning" to a passing cop, then engaging him in an idle conversation which was very flattering to the cop! He did it again and again. Chief Bolton, who had no fine diplomatic airs, cried, "That big-nosed bastard. Who the hell does he think he is? I'm the Chief of Police around here."

When the Chief's complaint came to Ira Groome's attention he called him in to him, just as he would have done on the bridge of his ship. "Yes, my friend, I've talked to your men," he said. On a quiet night on the North Atlantic when he was on the bridge, he said, a seaman strolling along the deck would come under his eye and he would call him up on the bridge and talk to him, saying provoking things, just to draw him out. Sound them out on everything in the world! And then you knew where a man really stood. His loyalties! Or the lack of any loyalty. Loyalty was the thing.

The policemen were very much like those seamen. The Chief nodded, he could see this, and he could see, too, that bit by bit he should get rid of the deadwood, the ones without deep loyalty and dedication to him. "Be utterly impersonal," he said to the Chief. "Never get personally involved, and then you can be utterly ruthless," and he made the Chief cough and clear his throat as if he had suddenly become aware that he himself was another faceless man in a uniform.

And a few weeks later Ira Groome did a wonderful thing for the Chief. An unhappy, disruptive relationship existed between the Chief and his deputy, Tom Frawlick. The deputy had complained to the commissioners that he had written dozens of memoranda to the Chief, all of which had been unanswered or ignored. The Chief said Frawlick was a paranoiac, and, anyway, the subjects of the memoranda had always been attended to. It was difficult for the commissioners to make a judgment on the matter. "Men who feel overlooked are a threat to any organization," Ira Groome warned his colleagues. "Beware of overlooked men. I take this seriously." On his own he made some enquiries, and then, encountering Tom Frawlick in the corridor one afternoon, he asked him to have a cup of coffee. They walked over to a drugstore just a block from the police building. Finding himself walking along the street with Commander Groome, Tom Frawlick was excited and on edge. There had been a heavy fall of snow. It was just two weeks before Christmas, and walking slowly through the snow they talked about little things. But in the drugstore Ira Groome began to talk about them all being in the service. In a sense, he himself was nothing, the deputy in himself was nothing. All that ever counted was a perfect and unimpeded enforcement of the law. He sounded so much like a stern, dispassionate old medieval pope talking to a monk from the provinces that Frawlick grew awed. A man who imposed his little personal problems on his superior weakened the general sense of service in the force. It was no time for little personal problems. A man who did this was the worm in the apple. Frawlick, a man of fifty with a wife, three children, and a mortgage on his home, got carried away by Ira Groome's magnetic faith. He knew the Commander was a well-remembered hero and a rich man. People expected such a man to tell them what to do, and now Ira Groome was saying quietly and sternly that a man could find freedom in perfect service. Sometimes a man performed this service with an act of abnegation, a thing done for the sake of the restoration of harmony.

21

Awed and carried away though he was, and knowing **Ira Groome** expected him to say he would resign, he kept his head. Tears came to his eyes, yet he waited shrewdly, and finally Ira Groome, changing his tone, said curtly, "I don't suppose there's any future for you on the force. Frawlick, you'll have most of your pension. Why don't you make yourself a buck? Why don't you go somewhere else?"

"Where do I go, sir?"

"Chief security officer at Continental Breweries."

"They don't know me, sir."

"They know me. I've talked to them. The same salary and you'll have your pension, too," and then they walked out in the snow.

It snowed for days and at the end of the week, when the deputy's letter of resignation came in, the Chief tried to express to Ira Groome his appreciation, his gratitude, and his own humble respect. He wasn't good at this. Fumbling the words clumsily he sounded fawning. Ira Groome cut him off with "Sir?", his head going back imperiously. This time the Chief seemed to know that "Sir" meant, "Are you insulting me by making this a personal matter? I'm not your pal, my good man." And after the silence Ira Groome started talking about his difficulty in getting adjusted to the cold winter weather after the salubrious sunny days in Brazil.

But soon he began to find the cold weather bracing. He liked Christmas at the Finley farm, with the logs on the great hearth and the Christmas presents, and the dinner, and the people dropping in for carol singing. Now a well-known figure around town, he was seen at hockey games in the Gardens, or at fights, always in a box with the same politicians with liquor-red faces who talked the brutal executive language of obscenities; and afterwards, going to a hotel, even if he was accompanied by the Mayor or the Attorney General he walked half a step ahead, and they fell in behind like junior executives or young officers who were honored to be carrying his bags.

Then one noontime in the middle of March when it was unexpectedly cold, he was crossing the City Hall square, on his way to the hotel across the street where he had a luncheon appointment. His handsome brown suede coat with the mink collar was draped over his shoulders like a cape, and since his leg wasn't bothering him and he didn't need the cane, he came striding briskly across the square in the strong March sunlight. In spite of the bright sun the great pool was still frozen. Children in toques and brightly colored sweaters skating around stopped suddenly to swirl and throw up sprays of ice. Then these children, there were eight of them, began to circle around the one elderly skater, an old man with a ratty fur hat and long flowing scarf, and one by one as the children swooped around the elderly man they gave his scarf a little tug; each time he nearly fell; then he saw that he was part of their game and he beamed and liked it, and each time a child touched his scarf he saluted with a broad old happy grin. Someone called, "Hey, Commander," and he turned. Leo Cawthra, who had also been crossing the square, was approaching him. He honestly didn't recognize Cawthra, who was white-haired and thin now.

"Leo Cawthra, Ira."

"Leo — after all these years, well, well, well," and he put out his hand. "You've lost weight, Leo."

"I'll put it on again."

"Well . . ."

"You look pretty good yourself, Ira."

"I'm quite fit. What do you do?"

"I do the column."

"Newspaper work, eh? Do you like it?"

"Ah, Ira, I see you don't read me. Well, you used to be quite a reader."

"Oh, I still read. Economics. History . . . the stuff I need."

"All the war memoirs too, I imagine."

"Of course, the war memoirs."

"I remember the days when we used to meet and almost the first question would be, 'What have you been reading?' Well, anyway, I see you don't read my column."

"I'll start tonight, Leo."

"Good," Cawthra said heartily, and waited, expecting to be asked how his life had gone, or about his home and whether he had any children, or had he time now for a drink. Shouldn't they get together for a drink? It was an awkward moment. The distance widened. Finally Cawthra laughed uneasily. Malice in his eyes, he said, "Well, I should have known it, Ira."

"Should have known what, Leo?"

"That you'd end up as boss of all the cops."

23

"Boss of all the cops," he said, his head going back as he appraised Leo with an almost magisterial concern. Then he smiled. It was a slow smile, very private in its cynical amusement. "That's very good, Leo," he said. "The boss of all the cops. Very good," and he gave him a pat on the shoulder. "You're a good man, Leo. Well, I'm late for an appointment," and he swept away, his fine open coat floating behind him. Crossing the street to the hotel, he entered the lobby, where he stopped suddenly at the foot of the escalator. He didn't know why he stopped.

Held there, he watched the faces coming down the escalator, coming down to him, as if this was the place named for his appointment, and he watched, waiting for one of those descending faces to light up in recognition. An old man? A young man? A girl? Yet so far all the faces were impassive in descending. Which one, and would he himself be recognized? He had to stand in sight so he couldn't be missed. Then, catching himself, he looked around in surprise. His appointment was with Sam Adelman who owned a string of taxis, and it was in the bar. He headed for the bar, shaking his head in wonder at himself.

FOUR ≋≋≋≋≋≋≋≋≋≋≋≋≋≋≋≋≋≋≋≋≋≋

That night Carol Finley was to come to his place after a dinner party. And when he was in the library waiting for her, Horler came in with the morning paper. "You'll certainly want to take a look at this, Commander," he said, and he sat down while Ira Groome read Leo Cawthra's column.

Cawthra knew how to take a story that gave him secret, sardonic satisfaction and, using the touch that made him so well loved, turn it into one of his self-deprecating, mocking tales. This column was his story about the city's distinguished Chairman of the Police Commission. In the war days, Cawthra and other young naval lieutenants had sat around in pubs trying to figure out what terrible thing had happened to their pal, Ira Groome. He had been a warm, friendly, open, easy-going fellow with soft blue eyes, an archeology student who was a bit of a poet, and he had a bright, laughing girl named Julia they all adored. Some bad things had happened to him early in the war. He had been wounded, and had been in a coma, close to death, for five days. On his first crossing after his hospital days, his vessel had been sunk.

And then had come the remarkable change in him, the incredible change! Before, he had been a very human guy, doing a job, and hoping it would soon end. But now his eyes, and even his posture, changed; he straightened up, he even managed to look heavier. Maybe he wore an extra sweater or two. And he turned strict on the seamen. He had no time for sentiment. The rhythms of his speech changed, too. He was crisp and impersonal. He began to win promotions, and soon, having won all the available decorations, he became the youngest commander doing convoy work, and no longer had any time to get involved with those aimless, undedicated, good-natured men who liked to sit ashore and talk about life. Cawthra himself felt pushed away. "What the hell happened to that bastard Ira Groome?" they all used to ask.

The last time Cawthra saw him was at the war's end when he was in Paris. Groome was in the Ritz, and was at the long bar among men with heavy gold braid, lapping up the champagne cocktails. Cawthra went to speak to him, but didn't. Ira Groome looked too important. Even when he laughed, he didn't let go for a moment.

Back in London, sitting in a pub, Cawthra talked to his friends about Ira Groome. They agreed that after the war Ira could have no future. In civilian life, out of uniform, he would be a duck out of water; he wouldn't be able to hold a job, he wouldn't know what to do with a wife and family. Yet Ira Groome married a lovely woman, he wrote. Ira Groome had a son, too. Cawthra didn't let on that he knew what had happened to Julia Groome and the son. Instead, he gave the story the endearing twist his readers loved. He wrote, "See what a fool I was? See what fools we all were? We wanted to know what terrible thing had happened to this man because he no longer wanted to be like us. What had happened to Ira Groome was that in the war he had been forging in the smithy of his soul" . . . Cawthra had shamelessly borrowed the phrase . . . "those great strong qualities that gave him his unbroken successes in the industrial world and made him rich and independent, and allowed him now, just out of the same old sense of dedication and service, to be Chairman of our local police commission."

When Ira Groome had finished the column, his chin cupped in his hand, he said nothing.

"What do you make of all that, Commander?" Horler asked.

"You remember Cawthra, don't you, Horler?"

"Yeah. The subie. Easygoing, wasn't he?"

"Leo Cawthra. And now that malice. What did I ever do to him? And when? And where? What's he trying to say to me?"

"That he got left behind, maybe."

"Or dropped. I don't remember ever having any reason for dropping Cawthra. I could sue him, or complain to the paper. I won't, of course, he'd be sure he'd got under my skin. When did we lose touch with Cawthra?"

"Sometime after we lost our ship, I think, sir."

"Cawthra with that ship? I don't think so."

"No, he wasn't. Sir, do you remember the two survivors with us on the ship? The girl and the big fellow. Wild ones, weren't they, sir? Gina what was her name?"

"Gina Bixby."

"And big Chone."

"Jethroe Chone."

"Stayed in my mind a long time, sir."

"Jethroe Chone. Yes, an interesting pair. A wild pair," he said, musing, as if after having put them out of his life and out of his mind for years he was now letting them come in on him. Gina Bixby, a tall fair girl of twenty, and Jethroe Chone, a big red-headed man of forty. Making the crossing from Boston to England their ship had been torpedoed, and the corvette had picked them up. Chone, a man of threatening, savage silences. And Gina Bixby — what was she? What was she?

Then he quickly blocked these figures out of his mind before he could dwell on them. It was as if he really couldn't remember any more about them. Right then indeed he couldn't. "It was too long ago, Horler," he said, shrugging. Suddenly that pain of things missed that he hadn't felt since he left São Paulo stabbed at him. Again there came sneaking into his heart before it could be smothered that São Paulo hunch about a pilgrimage to a place where he could learn why life had been passing him by. But he drew back, aghast that he could be touched by this kind of São Paulo nonsense again. This was not São Paulo . . . He was not bored here. He liked his work. Another place? What place, he scoffed . . . Gina and Chone were really out of his mind now . . . The world was full of places where disturbing things had happened to him.

Yet he said to Horler, "What was I like when I was a lieutenant?"

"When you were a lieutenant?"

"Right."

"Well, Cawthra was your pal then, wasn't he, sir? Cawthra would . . . " But they heard the doorbell. Quickly putting the newspaper out of sight on a bookshelf he thought he was really putting it out of his mind, too — as he did all things he couldn't bear to remember — and where they would stay unless touched by some enchantment.

Carol Finley could only come at these odd times, if she could get away, and on short notice. She liked it better when she could come there for brunch, with Horler cooking them a fine eggs Benedict which they would have with some white wine and some Mozart before they went to bed. In bed she was really more to his taste than Miss Meadows. Miss Meadows had a harvest-time fullness of figure that had a very quick attraction for him. But he told Carol, "You have really excellent breasts, old girl. A perfect breast should be of a size and shape that can be covered by a champagne glass without having the glass tip. You understand? A breast should have a vibrant life of its own."

"I see," she said. "Well, as long as I'm the best. Nothing but the best for you, Ira." But tonight, after he had slipped out of bed on the way to the bathroom, she called, "Hey, Commander."

She was lying on her side, her elbow on the pillow, her chin in her hand, the warm flush still on her neck and cheeks. She usually lay back breathing deeply with her eyes closed. He never remained beside her to talk and hold her and caress her idly. As she eyed him standing there, a distinguished figure even in all his nakedness, there was restless dissatisfaction in her face.

28

"What's the matter with me, Ira? Tell me," she said.

"The matter with you? What is this?"

"You hop up so quickly. You get away."

"Good heavens, Carol."

"I can almost hear you saying, 'I hope you understand, old girl there's nothing personal about this,' " and then she shrugged, "Don't you really like me, Ira?"

"Like you? Carol, you really satisfy me."

"I mean aside from this, this . . . satisfaction."

"Yes — well. I'll figure it out, Carol," and he grinned.

"But I know why I like you," she persisted.

"Why do you like me?"

"You're a monster."

"Me?"

"Of course," she said, sitting up in the bed. "I'll bet you don't throw a shadow when you're walking in the sunlight. And I know why."

"You do?" and he smiled. "Well, why?"

"You've no past, Ira."

"Oh, don't be absurd," he said a bit impatiently.

"And I know you are very lonely," she said. "Oh, I don't mind," she said with a secret smile as if she knew he was saving up all his loneliness for her, and her manner made him uncomfortable.

"I never had much time to be lonely," he began. But she cut him off gently, "Ira — I know your wife is dead. But you never talk about her, or about the life you led. Never at all. You never talk about your son. What's his name, Ira?"

"Chris," he began, "oh, I don't mind telling you about Chris . . . " and while he wondered where he should begin, there popped into his head a picture of himself and a middle-aged executive named Bronson, in his home in São Paulo. Late one night, Bronson was putting on his coat to leave, and Chris, then just fourteen, had come to the hall to say good night. Bronson turned affably to the boy: "Well, Chris, where do you want to go to school now?" And Chris answered solemnly, "I want to go to a military school."

"A military school?" Bronson repeated in surprise. "A military school? Why do you want to go to a military school?" Solemn and serious, Chris said, "Because I want the discipline."

"I see, I see," Bronson said, turning away awkwardly. Leaving, he said, " 'I want the discipline'. What a strange remark from a young boy. What's got into him?"

Now he could almost hear Bronson's voice. It hurt him. He knew that Chris was now far away from him, and he was bewildered by his sudden wild regret. What do you think? He looked helplessly at Carol. He wanted to go to her, to open his arms and tell her about his son, and how he missed him. Yet he couldn't. All the years of being utterly impersonal, the years of iron restraint, of discipline, were a suffocating grip on his throat. And he couldn't get the words out, he couldn't open his arms. It frightened him. "Why am I like this? What happened to me?" he thought desperately. His head sank, his lowered eyes were on his big bare feet, and he realized he was naked. And even more vulnerable. "Some time we'll talk," he said shortly. "Yes, some time we'll talk," and hurrying into the bathroom, he closed the door.

When they had both dressed and he had fallen back on his manner of easy comradeship, good hunting, good sportsmanship, they had a drink, then he took her out to her car. She liked to be at the farm before midnight and preferred to drive home alone. Standing on the steps he watched her car's red tail-light go down the drive, and turn, and when the light vanished he was relieved; he had been close to being shattered. The thing had been brushed aside and now he could give himself to his own work, and he walked briskly into the house. He had been preparing the yearly report on criminal activity in the city. Now he took his papers to his bedroom. The heavy window drapes and the chair were in deep burgundy, the wall-to-wall broadloom an oyster shade. The desk was of mahogany. In his sharkskin velvet dressing gown, he sat at this desk dealing with the statistics: the increase in the number of rapes, the number of crimes of violence, the break-ins, the murders and traffic violations . . . a comparison of these statistics with those of other cities on the continent. The assertion that his city was the best-policed city on the continent, the one city where a man could walk alone at night on the streets and not be mugged . . .

Suddenly he put down his pen and lay back in the chair, puzzled by some terrible dissatisfaction. Statistics! Murders, break-ins, rapes, muggings. Just impersonal statistics. The wild jungle whirl of life behind the statistics never came near him; he never saw the twitching face of the man with the knife hurling himself on the faithless woman who had just left her lover to become one of the statistics. Who was this man and his passion? And the daytime burglar, so dangerous because he knew the chance he took in the daytime. Who was that man? And the hitchhiking girl, stripped naked in the car, he never heard her wild shrieks of fear as they finished with her and tossed her out of the moving car. A statistical shriek. And then he was in no mood to go on with the report.

Taking from the shelf a book by John Kenneth Galbraith, he made himself comfortable in the chair. He could handle Galbraith. He liked handling Galbraith. Tom Mathews had said, "That speech of mine in the Bahamas, wiping the floor with Galbraith, that was Ira. I used him on Galbraith." But after reading for an hour he became unbearably restless and tossed the book aside. "Horler. Are you there, Horler?" he called.

When Horler, who had been dozing, came down the stairs, buttoning up his white jacket, he said, "How about a Scotch-and-soda, Horler?"

"Very good, sir."

"Bring one for yourself, Horler."

"With pleasure, sir," and when Horler came with the drinks he said, "Sit down, Horler. Tell me what's going on." Again they were keeping each other company late at night in the big house, making small talk. "Stevenson was asking about you," Horler said.

"Hmm. Who's Stevenson?"

"The third house along the street. He walks that English bull terrier. Brought it all the way from England. He asked if I thought you'd mind him dropping in."

"Stevenson? Where does the man come from?"

"Oh, he's all right. Got a rich father ninety years old who has a mistress. The one who was his nurse. The family hates her."

"Naturally. Hmm. Quite an old boy. The father, I mean."

"Yeah. The father. That dog of Stevenson's is a bad one," Horler chuckled. "You know that sheep dog along the street? A lovely gentle dog. That bull terrier tore a big gash in his throat. All hell to pay."

Sipping his drink, Ira Groome happened to glance at the

thin gray hair on Horler's head and the skin now loosening on
jowls that made his face heavier. His teeth, too, weren't good. Or
there was something the matter with his plate. Horler, the
stocky, fearless bosun. The thin, long bosun's whistle! Pipe secure! Oh, Horler would never go to pieces. "Well, if you've
finished your drink, Horler — now back to work for me," he
said. "By the way. Get your teeth fixed, eh? Send the bill to me."

When Horler was leaving with the tray, he gave him an
apologetic pat on the shoulder, for he knew that he had been noticing Horler's physical deterioration to mask a painful glimpse
he had just had of himself. Not physical deterioration in his
case. Nothing wrong with the shape he was in. No, something
more important. Something more interesting. It struck him that
his own life had been going downhill. Oh, for a long time, maybe
for many years, it had been going downhill. And he had known
it in São Paulo, and now he was full of wonder.

This should be amusing to him, he thought. Every man of
his age had this feeling. In every man's life there was a high
point, and from then on it was downhill all the way. Then why
was he so perplexed? The thing was . . . well, where had the high
point been? The great days when he had been called "Ribbons"
Groome, the dashing Commander? No! Nothing that banal!
Thank God he hadn't been one of those tiresome bored men
whose lives had been empty since the war days. Anyway, why
was he playing this introspective game? It could lead nowhere.
And yet gnawing away at him now was his certainty that his
high point had been somewhere before his business successes,
even before his war successes.

But this was absurd. How could there be such a high point
if he couldn't even remember it? It looked as if he was cooking
this up just to amuse himself. Yet . . . just the same . . . downhill
from where and when? And as he moved around the room,
pausing sometimes, his concentration became so deep it almost
hurt his skull. A voice should be there to remember. Whose
voice? Voices should be coming out of the walls, faces should be
in the light's pale glow on the ceiling. A voice from some room
in the many rooms of his life. Some shadow-hidden place in his
mind, suddenly bright and clear, and in that place a blending of
voices full of wild passion. Voices suddenly gentle; a place with
a life of its own. Out of all the places where he had been, whose

voice? São Paulo or Spain? The West, Japan, or Germany? And he stood in a trance, waiting, as if for the right enchantment to touch him.

Finally he got undressed and went to bed. Lying in bed in the dark, he waited for those moments that come just before sleep when a man can hear a hundred whispers. These were the secret whispers, and if they could be heard they could be trusted. Roman generals heeded these whispers the night before a battle. Mark Antony — the voices in the night before Actium . . . trust these voices. But he fell into a sound sleep that lasted till dawn. With the first streak of light coming through a cleft between the drapes he woke up, and lay a long time in that changing light. Finally he got up and stood at the window looking out at the street in the bleak light. Snow was still banked along the curbs. The snow plough had made a clean black ribbon out of the road. A lifeless morning. Down the street, and at this awful hour, came a man in a fur coat and woollen toque, walking a dog. His neighbor Hendricks. The fur coat thrown over his pajamas, the pajama tops tucked into galoshes. Dragged out of bed by the short-taken dog. The sheep dog. The one Horler said had been bitten on the throat by the bull terrier. "What the hell," he said, sighing, and turned away in disgust with himself.

Ira Groome bored with his life? So bored he took the time to concentrate on a man's pyjamas stuck in his galoshes? Yet he had everything a man could want. He had his own money. He had power and influence. He had women, and this lovely old house. And he recently had heard a man say good-naturedly that Ira Groome had such a sense of self-discipline he made other men feel demoralized. And he had his work! A splendid, useful service that was helping to hold a city together as a good place to live and raise children. And, above all, he had no messy personal involvement with anyone. No one could try and torment him and bring him pain.

As he went into the bathroom and got a glass of water, he drew on his cynical sense of humor; all men got bored, which was why they fought and killed and plundered. What other way out was there? What was even more astonishing was that the human race could go from generation to generation, men and women programmed to find each other mysterious, and doomed to grow bored doing the same things over and over again for

33

thousands of years. With these thoughts he got himself into a cynical, grim good humor. He went back to bed.

Yet he knew how boring tomorrow would be. And it was, right from the beginning. Right at his late breakfast time, Holden, the lawyer, telephoned, asking him to lunch so he could give some advice about a suitable speaker at a lawyers' convention on the theme "The Policeman in Court". "What a pity I have an engagement, Holden," he said quickly. Eating with the lawyer would mean listening to a hundred corny quotations from Tennyson. He would rather eat alone. That day he ate at the York Club in the sedate high-ceilinged dining room, a place where he could nurse his solitude. Yet he discovered that three businessmen he hardly knew were proposing to join him for coffee, and he became very remote. He frightened them away. That evening there was a dinner party at Tom Mathews' house. His dinner companion was a trust company president's wife whose conversation so numbed him that he kept saying, "Really. Really, you don't say," to keep himself awake. Till suddenly he became aware of her hurt eyes that told him she knew she was boring him, and he felt stricken. He could see what would happen if he went around town in this utterly unfamiliar frame of mind treating well-meaning people who had great respect for him with supercilious disdain. Next morning, before going out, he drank a tumbler of gin.

He had never been a heavy drinker. He despised people who drank heavily and let themselves get out of control, and then ran around offering grovelling apologies. For him gin had been the lightest of drinks, lighter than champagne or vodka. After he had swallowed the tumbler, he filled a silver flask. He did this when Horler was upstairs in his own room.

That day, moving around town, he had a cheerful word for anyone who spoke to him. He exuded an air of jovial well-being. At times he even felt elated. In a few days this elation had become so attractive, so irresistible, that he couldn't resist it, and each morning before he went out he took his tumbler of gin and filled his flask. And then he found that the sense of elation had deepened into another kind of feeling which fascinated him, a baffling sense of expectancy. An intimation that something lay ahead. Some encounter. Some event. No matter where he was, and no matter what company he was in, when this feeling hit

34

him he quickened. And he had a hunch that this was why he had left São Paulo — this was why he was here in town and had to remain here.

At the next meeting of the Police Commission he presided at the head of the table with even more than his usual majestic serenity. That day the Judge had a lot to say in his tart, gruff style, and Ira Groome, listening solemnly, would suddenly chuckle, and then laugh to himself and look at the Judge in surprise. It was as if he had just recognized that the Judge had a great deadpan humor. The Judge, who had never thought of himself as a sly wit, began to believe he indeed had a sly and subtle humor, and for the rest of the afternoon he kept beaming at Ira Groome. That same day, at the end of the meeting, Ira Groome took an appreciative interest in the Mayor's haircut and his too youthfully cut clothes. Stylistically he was very helpful in the advice he gave to the Mayor. But the hurt that came into the Mayor's eyes told him he had sounded patronizing. Ira Groome then suffered some loss of self-respect, and he clasped the Mayor's hand warmly. He could not go on like this, day after day, dragging himself down, making arrogant remarks to people. A disgrace was inevitable, he thought.

In the third week of his gin period, with only Horler aware of his problem, he told himself it was necessary to go away for a cure. This was a very hard thing for him to do. It meant forsaking the secret feelings that had been delighting him; the fine sense of expectation, the certainty that the expectation was to be satisfied by some encounter here in town. He told his colleagues and business friends a story about advice from a doctor; his mild heart condition required a little rest. The doctor had said he should hole up somewhere out of town for ten days or two weeks, and he went to Maplewood.

Maplewood, an expensive nursing home sixty miles away, was an old mansion in a park-like setting of elms and oaks, with lawns sloping away from the house to a lower ridge and brushland; and beyond the ridge was the wide lake. The house had a big, comfortable central lounge where the guests could meet. Many of them knew each other anyway. There were doctors, lawyers, advertising men, politicians. Some suffered from nervous breakdowns, one from a syphilitic collapse of the nervous system. But Ira Groome was listed as a heart patient in need of a rest. For twelve days he kept pretty much to himself in his comfortable room. When he returned to the city he was utterly free of fantasies and boredom. It was astonishing. He was Commander Groome again.

He got to be very good at timing his drinking bouts, although he couldn't figure out whether they came on because he was afraid of the terrible boredom, or because he felt some desperate need for that strange, quickening sense of expectancy. Again he wondered if he had had an intimation that the thing he expected would happen here in town.

In the next eight months he went twice more to Maplewood, but no one was any wiser, and he was encouraged on all sides to continue to look after his health.

FIVE

In October, when it was time to go again to Maplewood, he
put it off. For two weeks he had been deep in gin, yet having
luck around town. There was no doubt about it, he was courting
a disaster putting off the quick-healing journey, and he knew it.
He really knew it. And worse still, he felt good about putting it
off. Mrs. Finley's growing concern only irritated him.

"Now listen, Carol," he said sternly after she had come to
his house unexpectedly one night and found him dozing before
the television set. "There's no danger whatever of me becoming
an alcoholic. Be a good girl. Let me have my own little
problem."

"Ira, you've handled this thing so beautifully," she protested. "I don't understand why you put it off this time."

"Simple, my dear. Simple. One or two things have to be cleared up."

"Before you go?"

"I think so."

"But Ira, listen to me. A man like you won't be able to stand some disgraceful scene where you make a great fool of yourself and fall on your face. Please, Ira . . . when will you go?"

"Tomorrow. Or the next day."

"Promise me, Ira."

"I know what I'm doing," he said curtly. "Now just keep out of this, Carol."

He couldn't tell her that each day now his increasing sense of expectation had been filling him with youthful wonder. Nor could he tell her that he felt quite safe delaying his departure while nursing the expectation. At any time he could be whisked out to Maplewood; he had already been booked in there. Was it possible that he couldn't bear to be restored to his old sound frame of mind — so he could return and go on being their Commander Groome? And how amusing this idea was, he thought, and often smiled to himself.

Going around town, or driving with Horler, or attending some businessmen's hotel luncheon, he contained himself, remaining happily apart, as if he knew he had to be ready at any moment to recognize someone or some place. The recognition would have to come unexpectedly; it would be like a spontaneous act of creation, an unsought thing, a sudden enchantment.

Late one afternoon driving with Horler around Queen's Park, he said suddenly, "Stop a moment, Horler." Pressing his face against the car window, he watched a group of students: three girls in jeans, three big fellows, and another fellow who had grabbed a tall girl, hoisted her on his shoulders, and now stumbled and fell. This group saw that the Rolls-Royce had come to a stop and they stared. He stared intently at each face, as if expecting one of them to come forward. "Drive on, Horler," he said after a moment, and he smiled.

There had been other moments like this one, in hotels and bars when men and women caught his eye, and he had a hunch, as he had had in the park, which he treated afterwards with amusement, that he was delaying his departure to Maplewood because he knew he had to keep an appointment.

An appointment with whom? And where? A note made a month ago and misplaced? He had hundreds of appointments. Some of them he often overlooked until the last moment. But this one, again that awareness of a terrible failure of memory. Memory! Come on, come on, come on. If he went away to Maplewood now, then returned, his life in order, it might be too late. Come on, come on. So he was here in town at the time of Mrs. Finley's hunt and her party, and here too for another meeting of the Police Commission.

It was four-thirty in the afternoon, and sitting at the head of the long table he listened with the others to Chief Bolton, who was asking them to support his plea for the restriction of licences for massage parlors in the city's downtown core. The neighborhood was deteriorating. It was impossible to control the deterioration, with loudspeakers permitted to blare out the attractions of body rubs and porno shops. This pimp's paradise. This hooker's heaven. "Yes, it really distresses me," Judge Benton interjected. "You know I was born not far away from that neighborhood, just to the east. I can't believe it now." Sighing, he told about the fine families living there in the old days, and how as a boy he had walked on fine shopping streets now given over to body-rub parlors. Every day on his way to the university he had walked those streets. Well, he for one would do anything in his power to support a move to lift the quality of life in the neighborhood. "I'd like to see all that dreadful riffraff swept out into the streets. What do we intend to do, Commander?" "Yes, yes," Ira Groome said, nodding as if in deep meditation, his eyes on the long draped windows. The drapes were not quite closed. A street light skimming through the aperture held his eyes; he couldn't break his trance. A scene was growing in his imagination. A wild night scene. Worn-out old stores, massage parlors, beaten-up bars, and porno stores were disgorging all the disreputable, disorderly criminals, the naked girls, the ruthless young pimps, the fat old bookies, the thieves, and one or two crooked cops. They came out shouting, milled around, blocking traffic, then they all linked hands, and, laughing and screaming, whirled round and round an elderly old fairy in a blond wig, who shouted gleefully, "See Mother Benton, see, I'm to be queen of the May."

39

"Eh, oh quite true, quite true, Judge Benton," he said, clearing his throat importantly. The Judge, who had been waiting for his attention, also cleared his throat. "Excuse me, Judge, for one moment," he said, and got up and left the room. He returned quickly, too quickly for a man who had apparently gone to the washroom, for the hurrying had put a flush on his face. "Now gentlemen," he began, still standing, but then he coughed, he gagged, he choked, and the lapel of the Judge's coat was sprayed with gin. The sleeve of the Mayor's new suit was gin-sprayed too. Stunned and too outraged to speak, the Judge made a face at his lapel. The Mayor, mute in surprise, began flicking at his sleeve with his handkerchief.

Then their eyes, which had made him aghast for a moment, sank so deep into his pride that he stiffened and said with impressive dignity, "I'm very sorry, gentlemen. You see, I have a fever. I should be home in bed. I have the flu. Gin is not my drink, but I find that it lifts me, keeps me going. The only thing that can keep me going, and I'm not used to it."

"Gin?" the Judge spluttered, trying to control himself. "Straight gin?"

"Yes, straight gin."

"My father used to say that only English charwomen drank straight gin."

"My own father, sir, would have said the same thing. But if you should get the flu yourself . . . "

"The town is full of flu," the Mayor said helpfully.

"Yes, my wife has the flu," the Judge, gravely flustered, said. "You say you have a fever, Commander?"

"A little temperature. Yes. For days."

"I've noticed a flush on your face. See here, you're risking pneumonia, Commander. It's not the flu that kills. It's the pneumonia that follows."

"You should be home in bed, Commander."

"Well, I'm taking a two-week rest, starting tomorrow," he said.

"Good. You drive yourself too hard, Commander!

"Why don't you go right home now?" the Judge said quickly. He didn't want to catch the flu.

"You'd excuse me?"

"For heaven's sake, take care of yourself, Commander," the

40

Mayor said. "You're a tower of strength around here." So he left then. A secretary telephoned Horler. While he waited, he paced up and down, burning with humiliation. He had let the thing go on too long. He had courted this humiliation and had got it, even if he had bluffed his way out of the situation. Tomorrow, thank God, he could go to Maplewood. Then he went out to wait for the car and let his head clear. On the way home he made no conversation with Horler. At home he lay down; he slept for two hours. When he awoke he felt fresh and restless, yet firm in his resolve to leave town tomorrow. Horler had a good meal ready for him. He ate, then he indulged himself with his gin in a last gesture to his sense of expectation. He felt a little sad, as if he were walking out on something. He changed his clothes. He put on a dark suit. By nine o'clock he was in the car on his way to the Finley farm.

It was a cloudy night, but when the Rolls-Royce came along the highway by the white picket fence and turned into the Finley drive that ran through columns of poplar trees, the clouds broke, showing a bright full moon. As the car went slowly up the drive, he leaned out, examining all the poplar trees. Two weeks ago one of those poplars had died. It had been dry and bare and ugly. It had spoiled the look of the whole column of trees, and Mrs. Finley couldn't bear that it be seen by the members of her hunt. She had tried to have it replaced with another full-grown tree. Impossible. Far too expensive, her gardener said. Well, that old, dead tree wasn't going to be an eyesore for her party, she said.

"Let's see, Horler, if she really got that big tree replaced," Ira Groome said. "See if we can pick it up in the headlights." The car went forward slowly, then they backed up a hundred yards, then forward again as they tried to pick out the tree. "I can't believe it. I can't believe she got a new tree," Ira Groome said. "Let's get out of the car," and he said, "Come on, Horler, look for freshly dug ground around the trees." They went half-way up the drive, groping around. Two mystified figures standing in the drive. The earth was unbroken, it was all unbroken. "My God," he said suddenly, standing with his hands on his hips in the car's headlights. "She said she might have to do it and she did it. She's had that whole goddamned dead tree painted, Horler. That woman's crazy."

"No, just rich," Horler said.

"But to paint it."

"She could have sprayed it with paint."

"Should we go back and look for a sprayed tree, Horler?"

"I'd say to hell with it, Commander."

"Quite a woman, eh, Horler?"

"I'd say so, sir."

"Horler, I want your opinion. Can old trees or an old man ever branch out again?"

"A tree or a man. Very much the same," Horler said profoundly, and they got back into the car.

Ahead, on a gentle rise of land, was the old stone farmhouse with its white trim, the windows now a blaze of light. The house had two big new stone wings added to it. The moon was now so bright it held the house in a great wide silver glow. Off to the left, deep in the shadow, were the barns and stables. To the right of the house, and as far as the wooded ridge, the field was all one strange silver glow. The wide field was held in a silver sheen, banked by low hills all in deep shadow rising around the wide field. A bowl of light. No moving shadows to break it now. The hunters had gone. The grooms had loaded the horses into the vans. The hunters had moved into the house for the great buffet, and some of them had gone home, or they had come back with friends, for on this day Mrs. Finley held open house. Cars were parked around the circular drive.

Letting himself in, Ira Groome sauntered across the hall with its English prints and its oak panelling, and then he stood near the entrance to one of the large rooms in a new wing. The whole wing was a bit of old manorial England: dark panelling, gold-framed oil paintings, logs burning on a great hearth, and a long table near the hearth gleaming with white linen and silver dishes heaped with food. Liveried servants went back and forth from this table with drinks for the thirty guests who stayed on — company presidents, their wives in Pucci prints. The servants from the Hunt Club knew each guest by name: the same liveried servants were used at all the parties. It was a family thing. Only three of the hunters in their pinks had remained there; they were far down the room by the window. A sense of ease and well-being filled the room, for each man knew what the other was worth in dollars and cents, and how much he would come into. So they knew what to talk about; who had been in Spain, who was back from the Caribbean, who had a story about restaurants in the South of France, who could tell about the price of things in London. Everyone was rich, everyone loved horses, everyone was a little drunk, but no one was as drunk as Ira Groome.

Standing there in his new state of reckless benevolence, he suddenly had one of those hunches that had become so beguilingly important to him. These prudent, cautious, pleasant people with their benign expressions might have lots of little secret nervous quirks, or hidden, kinky tastes, but they had no real passion. Therefore they weren't his own people, and so he didn't belong here. The hunch surprised him. For years and years he had served them coolly and ruthlessly and had taken rich rewards; and to think now that they weren't his own people was dismaying. Where on earth were his people? And even as he asked this question, he felt himself lifted happily and swept away to dark places where he shivered, hearing wild cries and defiant curses, and saw faces twisted in passion. And he would have believed he was a little drunk if Angus McMurtry hadn't come along, sudden life in his dead face, as if he remembered saying that in Ira Groome's presence he felt more secure. It was plain that he wanted to feel strength in someone he trusted. McMurtry had been deposed by his own board of directors; it was a local social scandal, a much-talked-about thing. Everyone knew McMurtry couldn't live without his bank, there had never been anything else in his life. It was no wonder he was now in the first days of his nervous breakdown; in fact his lonely death was already plain to see in his gray face. His hand had come out eagerly, "How are you, Commander?" and he held on to Ira Groome's warm hand.

"Very well. Very well indeed," Ira Groome said, trying to free his hand. "And you, McMurtry?"

"You know what it's like these days," McMurtry said. "It's all around us. No values. No loyalties. Just grab!" He looked around and let himself go as if at last he had found an old friend. In fact they had never had an intimate conversation.

"Ruthless sons of bitches. Ingrates . . . Small-minded men . . . I can say this to you . . . " and then suddenly, "What's the matter, Commander? Are you missing someone?"

"Ah," he said, taken aback, "No. Why?"

"You keep looking around. Is it Carol?"

"Ah, yes, Carol."

43

"Down there . . . "

"It's all right, McMurtry," he said gently, touching his arm as he left him. "Rail now at the world if you want to. But at least you know when you had your innings," and he headed for Alfred, the smiling bartender, who knew them all so well. There he stopped, concentrated, then again looked around expectantly.

"Someone you're looking for, Commander?" Alfred asked. "Who?"

"I'm looking for a drink, Alfred."

"What are you drinking, Commander?"

"Gin, Alfred. Gin."

"Gin? Really? It was always brandy at this hour."

"Changing my luck, Alfred," and he laughed.

This laugh and his new restless, eager expression, which these people would never have associated with him, drew them to him. Acquaintances who had never felt at ease with him were comforted now by his dreamy smile and came over to him. There was plump, pink Perkins just back from Palm Beach, looking so wonderfully well preserved, and Jenkins — chinaware and toilets — goodhumored now and full of jokes, and Hubert Endicott, the hardware man, the head of all the rich Endicotts and their foundation. Hemmed in, he smiled and caught bits of conversation as he looked around. "Things haven't really changed in England. Only on the surface. Don't bother living there unless you have a title," and then, "This creeping socialism," and Mrs. Endicott whispering to Mrs. Jenkins, "Good heavens, Henry Perkins is sensual. I could tell by the feel of his fingers on my arm." "What is the point of trying to put aside something for your children?" "Creeping socialism." Then Carol, who had been hidden by three tall men, still in hunting pink, moved, and he saw her in her red silk dress sheathed with open black lace, looking lovely as she beckoned. But over there at the window he saw a young tall blonde girl in riding breeks. A restless, beautiful girl looking out the window, waiting and watching. Suddenly she moved into the shadows and vanished. His curiosity quickening, he moved over to the window. What had she seen out there that told her it was time to go? And he pushed back the drape and looked out at the great black pool of shadows around the moon-silvered field almost glowing in the dark. Like the sea! Except that a silver strip would be shimmering on the dark sea.

44

He really had to sit down. The last drink Alfred had handed him had been rather stiff. Sauntering out to the hall to the stairs, he went up six steps and sat down. When he looked up, Carol was at the foot of the stairs. "Are you all right, Ira?" she asked.

"Of course I'm all right," he said impatiently.

"How drunk are you?"

"Drunk? I'm not drunk at all. Good heavens, old girl."

"Well," she said, sighing. "I must say that no one gathers that you are drunk. You're wonderful, Ira."

"It's simple. It's everyone else that's a little drunk, my dear."

"Have you ever seen me drunk?" she said, sitting down three steps below him.

"Never. Or always. There you are. I don't know."

"I've been watching you, Ira. What's bothering you? Was there someone you expected to be here?"

"Well, you know something?"

"What?"

"I never wanted to be a cop," he said, almost innocently.

"Good Lord, Ira," she said. "You're not a cop. Don't be ridiculous."

"Police and police work. All over the world, and I'm in on it."

"But why is it so distressing?"

"I used to read books, I mean poems," he said. Suddenly there were tears in his eyes. "Eliot and Yeats . . . 'I made myself a coat of many old embroideries'. See. Yeats. I was twenty-four."

"I would like to have known you then. What were you then?"

"A lieutenant."

"A lieutenant. A young lieutenant. I wonder if I'd know you."

"I wonder if I would myself," he said. "I mean if he came walking in here now. Well, I wonder. Well," and he got up and took the few steps down the stairs where he stood looking around and wondering.

"I'm going to get Horler to take you home," she said.

"Might as well," he said.

"I'll go in and get you tomorrow. I'll drive you to Maplewood."

45

"No such thing, old girl. I'll drive myself. I always drive myself to Maplewood, don't I?"

"Let Horler drive you."

"My dear, I refuse to be dropped off like an old crate. I'll drive myself, as is my custom."

"Let me meet you there at noon. Let's have lunch there."

"If it gives you any pleasure, fine, my dear," he said indulgently. "Now where's Horler?"

He slept in the car all the way home.

SIX ~~~~~~

After sleeping in the car, he couldn't go right to sleep again at home, so he lay awake asking himself coldly what really bothered him about going to Maplewood to sober up. Was he, a grown man, willing to risk his reputation going around town nursing a gin-haunted fantasy that if he left for Maplewood he would be leaving behind an encounter with someone who had some knowledge of his destination. It was absurd. The risk was absurd. He had lived his life avoiding such risks, in protecting others from such risks. Ever since the war days he had been a screener of men who might upset the corporate service. The oil company's director of personnel, then the Brewers' Association's

47

staff under his discipline: each man nothing in himself, men who risked capital, but had never risked death together. All secure, sir. Pipe secure. Officer of the corporation. Officer of the watch. A prudent man. Prudence in the heart makes cowards of us all.

As he was saying these things to himself, he heard another little voice, "Don't turn your back on this one." "To hell with this," he said aloud, and he got out of bed. Without turning on the light, he went tip-toeing down the stairs, keeping close to the wall on the steps so they wouldn't creak and wake Horler. In the library he sat down in the New England rocking chair that was so easy on his back, and the strained muscles there; the old wound in his knee, tightening up sometimes when he walked, altered his balance because he wouldn't sacrifice his erect posture and firm stride.

Rocking back and forth, he grew disgusted with the weakness of his vacillation and picked up the telephone. He knew that Carol Finley did not sleep with her husband. A call in the night would not embarrass her. She might even be awake.

The telephone rang and rang, and then she answered, "Yes," very sleepily.

"Carol . . . "

"Ira . . . " and she was suddenly wide awake.

"I want to save you a little trip."

"Ira — Where are you?"

"No. Listen. I hoped to get you before you fell asleep. I didn't want you to get up in the morning and head for Maplewood. I'm not going, Carol."

There was a long silence. Finally she said quietly, "Are you all right, Ira?"

"Of course I'm all right."

"Have you been drinking?"

"I have not been drinking."

"Ira, are you drinking now?"

"Now really," he said angrily, "I haven't had a drink since I left your place."

"Honestly, Ira?"

"My dear, don't contradict me."

"Wait. Look . . . I believe you . . . Ira."

"Thank you, my dear."

"But what changed your mind?"

"I'm not an old drunk. I never was. I can't keep on making these trips. And furthermore, I won't."

"It's only a few days, Ira. It works, then you're great."

"Cut it out, Carol."

"Ira . . . Ira, are you there?"

"I'm here."

"You frightened me . . . "

"Oh, for God's sake."

"You've told people you're taking a little rest. You've told your colleagues. What'll they say?"

"I don't know that I care."

"My God, Ira, no one in the world cares as much as you do. It's why you never let anyone down. You can't now. It wouldn't be you. It's only a few days anyway, Ira. Ira — Ira." And suddenly her pleading tone made him feel his stubbornness was proof to her that he was in trouble. This worried him. "Take it easy, Carol. Look, I'll think it over," he said.

"And you'll let me know?"

"I'll let you know. Good night," he said. Yet as soon as he had put down the phone, there came welling up in him feelings that must have come out of vaguely remembered things in other places he had turned his back on. He turned out the light abruptly. He put the whole thing out of his mind, which he could do because he had long training at this trick. In bed again, he told himself he was exhausted, and he fell asleep.

Just before dawn when the telephone rang, he swung his arm in the dark and knocked the phone cradle off the bedside table. "Yeah," he mumbled.

"Are you all right, Ira?" Carol asked.

"Oh God, Carol."

"Are you all right?"

"What is this?"

"Just tell me you're all right."

"I'm all right."

"You haven't been drinking?"

"Carol — Carol. This is exasperating."

"You were to let me know."

"In the morning . . . in the morning."

"You'll call me in the morning?"

"First thing in the morning."

"And you won't take a drink."

49

"Let us cut this out, Carol," he said curtly. "Look, I'll meet you at Maplewood as we planned, right? Right!" In stiff control of himself he put down the telephone, turned out the light, went to sleep, was up at nine in the morning, had his breakfast, and was impatient with Horler. But Horler understood the impatience. He suffered seeing the Commander go off on these belittling journeys.

"Look after things, Horler," he said.

"You'll call me, Commander?"

"Tomorrow. What about that cleaning woman? Is she working out?"

"She takes too long in each room, Commander."

"Do you still give her the beer for lunch?"

"Two bottles. Says she needs the two bottles."

"Cut it down to one unless she works faster. Good luck, Horler."

"I'll be waiting to hear from you, Commander."

"Tomorrow," he said, waving his gloved hand. The car then circled the drive, going slowly along the side streets, then down the hill to the ravine and along the ravine road to the expressway that led up to the highway.

Early this morning there had been an hour of sunlight, then it had clouded up. The clouds now were low and heavy and it was getting darker.

He liked driving on open highways, he liked leaning back, his face impassive, nothing on his mind as he became one with the soft purr of the car. But this morning with heavy rain-filled clouds pressing down on fat farmland that now looked brown and bleak, he felt the loneliness of October. The renovated farmhouses taken over by city people were starkly neat and clean, but there were no cows in sight. He wanted to see cows grazing by a pond, as he used to see them when he was a boy. Drops of rain began to splash against the windshield. The deeper he got into the countryside, and the farther away from the city, the lonelier he felt, and the rain kept falling, and it got even darker. By noontime he had reached Maplewood grove and the big lodge by the lake. The water looked rough. There were white caps on the waves.

Turning up the drive, he parked his car and strode in to the lounge, said "Hello there," curtly to the desk attendant, then saw Carol coming toward him in a denim pantsuit, a pale heliotrope denim she had got from Paris. Her smile was casual, but he saw the relief in her eyes.

"Right on time, Ira," she said.

"A lack of punctuality is not one of my inadequacies."

"Are you hungry, Ira? You must be."

"Not really. No."

"I thought we might have a bite in the room. I ordered a lunch."

"Why not," he said, looking around the lounge. It was like a clubroom now to him, most of the club members there. He recognized Joel Ogilvie, the broadcaster, and Steven Parkinson, the broker, and Reggie Wilks, the great political fund raiser. From each one of them, as they caught his eye, he got the most courteous smile. If Carol had not been with him, they would have come to him with their hands out, hands always there to clasp his hand warmly. Yet their smiles stabbed at his pride even more painfully than the relief that had shown in Carol's eyes had done. Then Dr. Martin, middle-aged with rimless glasses and real gentleness in his face, came, and as he shook hands, his eyes asked, "Have you taken a drink or two this morning?" If he hadn't taken a drink, and if they could keep him away from the gin bottle for three or four days, there would be no problem. Everything would come easily. One more difficult period overcome, and back to his post he would go, as masterful as ever.

His room was like a very comfortable hotel room, and Carol, too, was at home in this room. On her instructions, a table with a white linen cloth had been moved in. Everything looked just right because they were willing to pay to have it look just right. "Your concern is beautiful, Carol," he said. But as they ate he became aware of the glint of satisfaction in her eyes. She ate and smiled, and ate and smiled again. Her satisfaction upset him. This kind of satisfaction could not come from love of him, he thought. Nor could his respect for her concern come from love. They were there out of a shared sense of keeping up appearances, though he knew he should not be there at all.

"Ira, you're not drinking your coffee," she said.

"I feel like a complete fool," he said.

"Here. Have some hot coffee."

"Thank you. I will."

"It's just the usual routine thing, Ira."

"I don't think so, Carol."

"Ira . . . "

"You don't get the point," he said restlessly. "I think this is just a way of trying to brush off something. A man brushing things off instead of trying to understand his own life."

"I don't know anyone who understands his life," she said in surprise, "Do you?"

"I'd like to, yes."

"Really? I don't think I'd want to. No, I'd feel it was the end of me."

"Maybe so," he said, then he felt himself pulling away from her and wondered if there was anyone around who could let him pour out his heart.

"You see, Ira, you stand for something," she said. "You really do. We all owe something to what we stand for, don't we?"

"What's that?" he said sardonically. "A lack of passion?"

"Ira — if you haven't seen," and she was hurt, "If you haven't felt . . . "

"Carol, you're wonderful in bed. Indeed you are, Carol," he said gently, as if she didn't know what he was talking about. And when he went to the window to watch the rain, he must have made some nervous movement, or shown something in his changing face that alarmed her.

"Ira," she said sharply.

"Yeah," he said turning. "Where's my coat?" Ignoring her as she stood up angrily, he went to the closet and got his coat and put it on and picked up his bag. He had taken three steps to the door before she grabbed his arm, her jaw thrust out.

"You're not going to do this, do you hear?" she said.

"Oh, get out of the way," he said.

"I've come here, Ira. I respect you, Ira, . . . "

"Please . . . " he said, his eyes on the hand gripping his arm, his eyes and his tone so commanding that she faltered. She let go his arm. "Thank you," he said crisply and strode to the door.

"Damn you, come back here," she cried, half in tears. When he didn't even turn, opening the door, she yelled, "Come back here, you bastard."

His back to her, he stood in a trance, not sure for a moment that he had heard the voice, not even sure where it had come from. Then, turning slowly, full of wonder he stared at her as if trying to make her out. He was frightening her. Raising his hand placatingly, he repeated softly, "*Come back here, you bastard. Where did that come from? Her very words.*"

"I'm sorry," she said, shaken. "It's so hard to get to you."

"Yeah," he said, still wondering. "If it had sounded a little wilder . . . "

"I'm exasperated, Ira. Oh, Ira, I'm not wild."

"And I'm not Jethroe Chone."

"Jethroe Chone? Who's Jethroe Chone?"

"Big Jethroe Chone," he said softly.

"Who the hell was Jethroe Chone?"

"A gambler," he said vaguely, still half in a trance. "A criminal. A wild man . . . "

"A friend of yours?"

"A friend? Hell, no."

"Someone you've met in your police work?"

"What? No — No."

"No, eh? And the girl," and she shrugged. "This 'Come back here' girl — the wild one not like me —"

And then, as he remained far away from her, her tone changed and she tried to get his eyes. "Ira — all along have you had a girl tucked away somewhere?"

"What? Oh, come off it," he said. He had put his bag down, lost in his own thoughts. He was slowly taking off his coat and tossing it at the bed. He sat down; then, becoming aware that she was waiting, he shook his head apologetically. "Things pop into a man's head as a voice sounds like — or words sound like," he said, trying to put her off, yet waiting for her to ask, "Whose voice did it sound like?" But she saw how reflective he was, and how he was making no further move to leave. Too wise to break into his thoughts, she sat down, sat with him in the silence. Finally she took off her shoes, and curled up her legs under her on the chair. Not a word was said. An hour and more passed.

"I really have to get back home, Ira," she said finally. "Ira, you're sure you're all right?"

"Of course I'm all right, Carol."

"I know you are," she said. "Now I'll have to drive in that damned rain. I wish it would stop."

"Take it easy," he said. "Drive carefully."

53

"You know me," she said. "Well, so long, and bless you, Ira," and she kissed him.

"So long. And Carol — dear Carol — thank you." And as soon as she had gone he turned back to the window and to the reverie that had been giving him such a feeling of lightness and wonder. He looked through the curtain of rain across wide lawns and trees to the lake. It was getting darker, and in the falling darkness the sky and the lake became one vast gray sea. The bare trees floated like shadowed ships there in the mist, and the rain seemed to bring the sea washing around him. Over to the left on the highway a light appeared, then another moved away, then vanished, while the sea swirling around lifted him up then tossed him down.

Then, looking around the room in surprise, he stood up slowly. He got his coat and put it on, he got his bag too, from the closet. He walked out briskly. He went downstairs to the lounge. With his air of great authority he spoke to Maloney, the attendant.

"Tell Dr. Martin, I remembered I had an appointment," he said curtly.

"I'll call the doctor. Please, just a minute, Commander."

"Don't bother," he said.

"Sir . . . "

"That'll do, Maloney," he said and walked out into the heavy rain. As it hit the back of his neck he pulled his coat high on his neck, then he strode across the parking lot to his car and turned on the lights.

As soon as he got on the highway he knew he had done the right thing, and his grim satisfaction changed to a lightness of heart. He wanted to get home, he liked the feeling of coasting along through sheets of rain. The mist was so heavy that the lights in farmhouses were mere fading pinpoints, and the closer he got to home the more buoyant his expectations became. His strong headlights easily picked out the white line on the road. He passed through towns. Twenty miles from the city he decided he should stop at the next gas station, call Horler, and tell him he was on the way home and to have a dinner ready. On the long curve, before he got to the bridge over the river, he saw the truck lights come out of the mist, then the truck skidded, it swung over to his right, truck lights in a blinding blaze, then the

54

monstrous impact, and then just the roaring in his ears before heavy blackness pressed down on his head, and his car, crashing through the railing, rolled slowly down, cracking and cutting off small trees on the slope. The car rolled three times, then settled upright in the valley with a thump, his headlights smashed, the car hidden in the valley by the heavy mist and rain.

Up on the highway a car's headlights shone from the place where the rail had been smashed, and this beam at that angle merely made a halo over the valley. Then other headlights from other cars, till that part of the highway was a bowl of light. Two men came sloshing their way down the embankment. A cop's motorcycle headlight, shining down the slope, picked out the car. The cop's voice on his radio; other voices began to shout, "Hello, hello, hello."

But it was half an hour before they got him out of the car, onto a stretcher, and up the hill and into the ambulance. Then, from a distance he heard the ambulance men talking, just a blur of voices, and he knew he wasn't dead. He wasn't sure. After the descending blackness — how long after he didn't know — there had been a soft, widening white light around him, putting him at ease, but this white light had gradually faded, and now he heard the voices. He felt intense pain in his jaw, and a terrible weight on his chest.

They took him into the city to emergency at St. Michael's, the downtown hospital. He was wheeled into one of the emergency cubicles. A curtain was whipped around him. They got his coat off, and got out his identification cards. "Good God, the Chairman of the Police Commission," someone said. The word was passed along. The nurse at the desk called his home. She got Horler, who said he would be right down himself, the Commander did not have a wife or family.

Two doctors were working on Ira Groome's broken jaw. His mouth was full of blood, but they knew it was not from the jaw. They were putting bandages on him while trying to get Dr. Onslow, a surgeon, on the telephone.

Horler came to the emergency desk. Gray-faced, fumbling his words, he tried to supply the necessary information to a girl at a typewriter who typed very patiently while he gripped the edge of the desk. "Who is the next of kin?" she asked, and he explained that the Commander's wife was dead, and his son some-

where in Africa. As for the ones who should be immediately no-
tifed — Horler went to speak, then hesitated. No name would
come to him. No one who should come rushing there as someone very close and dear to the Commander. No one. Then he
said, "Oh, yes. Mrs. Finley," and giving them her address, he
was rather sedately squeamish about it. After all, she was a married woman. "Oh pick out any goddamned big name," he said.
"The Mayor, the Lieutenant-Governor. Look, can't I see the
Commander? He'll want to see me. I tell you he'll want to see
me," he said threateningly.

"Now just relax," the girl said, and called a nurse who went
to the cubicle, then returned followed by a young doctor with a
beard. Horler said, "The Commander. How is he?"

"Take it easy," the doctor said. "You may be able to see
him."

Horler sat down within reach of the desk and facing the
street where the ambulances came in. At nighttime the emergency ward in this downtown hospital was a terrible place to put
a man like the Commander, and as Horler was thinking this with
his stiff, grim air, a skinny gray-haired drunk came wandering in
singing. A nurse scolding a junkie led him to the street door and
threw him out. The junkie immediately returned. He tried to
grab the nurse by the hair. Two security men came rushing
along the corridor. Then two cops came in with three hand-
cuffed, bleeding prisoners, who sat down beside Horler. An old
guy coming in claimed he had had forty dollars when he had
been in there an hour ago. A security guard grabbed him.

Then a troubled young doctor who had come along the corridor from the cubicles called diffidently, "Mr. Horler," and
looked around.

"Here, sir."

"You could see him now."

"Is he conscious?"

"I think so."

"Did he ask for me?"

"Yes, he did — now just for a few minutes, you understand," and he led Horler down the aisle.

"Doctor," Horler whispered before the doctor could open
the curtain that was around the cubicle. "What's the danger?
What's he up against?"

56

"There's some very bad internal bleeding," the doctor whispered. "His chest is smashed up. He may hemorrhage. Well, we have to see what we can do," and he opened the curtain.

In Ira Groome's bandaged head, the eyes were just slits in the bandages, yet he recognized Horler and blinked his eyes. He was trying to whisper. "Commander, I'm here," Horler said. Ira Groome couldn't move his jaw. Words finally came, "Well, Horler." He was moving his hand. He took Horler's hand. He couldn't see the sober, desperate anger in Horler's eyes, or the tears that came suddenly streaming down Horler's face, yet he knew Horler was there and he wanted him to know that his presence buoyed him up. His own thoughts now were clear. Images were dancing around in his head. "It's astonishing, Horler, I can remember everything now, everything," he whispered. "Everything now in the greatest detail."

"Take it easy, Commander," Horler said huskily, but after saying it he had to clear his throat. There was a long silence. Ira Groome, under the enchantment now, and with the old seaman's hand in his, felt himself racing away. The whole sea came rising up to him, and never had his perceptions been so acute and warm. "Close to the sun again," he whispered. "Close to the sun." As he felt Horler's grip tighten, the sea again washed around him, then he peered into the water in vast, satisfied surprise.

SEVEN 〜〜〜〜〜〜〜〜〜〜〜〜〜〜〜〜〜

There he was, Lieutenant Ira Groome, on the bridge at night. The ship, rolling on the sea's dark, undulating belly, made him lurch, and heavy spray-filled wind hit his face, but his eyes remained on the lookouts: one perched in the crow's nest, one on the bridge wing. He couldn't make out their figures against the black, unbroken sky till the ship dipped. Then he saw them shadowed against patches of light on the water when the great white-crested waves broke. Nothing could be seen out there in the darkness, not one of the sixty ships in convoy, all hidden, but keeping to their lanes; yet the bridge wing lookout, knowing he was being watched, stiffened alertly. The W.T. operator came up the ladder to hand him a signal. "I can't see it," he said, peering at the paper. The operator said, "H.Q. has lost three ships."

The squat, square figure at the voice tube, the Captain, turned to him. "Sir, submarine report," he said. "The convoy ahead has lost two ships, sir."

Captain Mallard, called "The Duck", said quietly, "And that means we'll soon be in the zone," and as he moved away from the voice tube to enter the asdic hut, a narrow slit of light fell across the bridge. When he came out he was in the slit of light again, moving over to the radar cabin. These slits of light, appearing so suddenly, then vanishing, deepened the blackness that followed. At the voice tube now, the Captain gave his quiet steering instructions. He was unruffled, solid, and so naval. Yet, like most of the corvette officers on the North Atlantic, he wasn't really naval at all. He had been a high-school history teacher.

Without turning from the voice tube he said, "Woodruff ought to be all right now. Take a look at him." Woodruff, the sub-lieutenant, who had been lying down for fifteen minutes in the wheelhouse on the couch where the Captain himself usually slept, had cynical eyes and a plump baby face. He had picked up ptomaine poisoning on his leave. Seeing Groome, he sat up, grinning. "All right now, Ira," he said.

"And I'll get a little sleep," he replied. In a few minutes he expected to be in his own little cabin, sound asleep. He went back to the Captain. "Woodruff's all right now, sir," he said. As he turned and trotted down the slippery steel steps, a voice came out of the darkness, "Still refusing to back down those ladders, eh No.1?" It was the navigator, Jackson, an Englishman with a beautiful quiet possession of himself. "I do what my father taught me to do. Back down ladders and don't break your neck."

"You didn't believe all he taught you, or you'd have kept away from the sea."

"True, Ira, true. Sleep well."

Going along the deck he grabbed at the rail as the ship slid down a deep gully. In the pitch dark he made out a figure at the rail bending over, gripping the rail with both hands as he vomited over the side. Horler, the bosun; after twenty crossings Horler still got seasick.

Wiping his mouth with his wet hand, Horler said, "It's always this way the first rough night out, then it doesn't happen again the rest of the crossing. I don't understand it, sir." His toque had fallen off. It was in the water at his feet.

"Well, what does it matter, Horler?" he said. "Take it easy." He picked up the toque and put it on Horler's head and clapped him on the shoulder. "All right now?" he asked.

"Yeah, okay," Horler said awkwardly, "Yeah, fine. Yeah, thanks." An officer picking up a seaman's toque, being concerned about him. That sort of personal interest, so typical now of Ira Groome, was very unusual in the services. An officer was supposed to be impersonal, utterly impersonal; only the thing they all did together was important. Horler tried to make out the Lieutenant's face in the darkness. "Are you all right yourself, sir?" Horler asked. "How do you feel now you're back with us?"

"Great, Horler," he said and laughed. A month and a half ago, returning with ships that had formed up at Londonderry, a stray wildcatting plane had come down, raking three of the four ships. Keeping away from the destroyer, it had come low over the corvette. Two seamen at the bow were hit; he saw them from the bridge. As he started down the ladder, he had been hit in the knee; he spun, and fell and cracked his head on the steel plates. He had a severe concussion. They had been afraid of brain damage. A day from Halifax he moved his big toes, then the fingers of his right hand. The sick-bay attendant shouted. He opened his eyes and knew he was alive, looking up into the faces of three seamen, each face wonderfully distinct. Men with their own faces, each face to be marvelled at, the face of a man who had his own life in a wonderful private world of his own. The wonder of each one of them astonished him. His eyes filled with tears.

EIGHT ≋≋≋≋≋≋≋≋≋≋≋≋≋≋≋≋≋≋≋≋≋≋

By morning the sky and the sea sparkled, and all day ships remained in their lanes keeping their smoke down. Since it was only the second day out, the hands were singing and joking and he was feeling exhilarated himself, and when night came and he should have been asleep in his cabin he came on deck to get a little air. In the cloudless night the sky with the new full moon was a great saucer of stars, the stars made small by the brightness of the moon. On deck it was almost as light as day. He could see the Captain's square face, he could even see the gold stripes on the Captain's sleeve. It was one of those nights when the corvette was a shining silver ship on a glowing, painted sea.

From this port rail where he stood, he could count six cargo ships. A trailing U-boat could count those ships, too. Yet no U-boat on such a night could surface and be hidden. Nothing could be hidden tonight. Held by the silver glow throwing silver ladders on the water, he watched, then suddenly stiffened in amazement. Out there in the vast glowing crystal bowl he saw it. Hanging there in the night was a room, a night-club room; and in this room was a table with one empty chair. Then the whole room sailed grandly by and vanished.

"Jesus Christ," he said. And Woodruff, who had been coming along the deck, heard him and was alarmed. "What's up, No. 1 ?"

"Out there — "

"What's out there?"

"Well — " and he laughed awkwardly. "The damnedest thing I ever saw in my life. Out there, floating grandly by, all lit up . . . Do you know Montreal? Do you know the Samovar, the old night club on Peel Street? There it was, Woodruff."

"Really?"

"There it was."

"Yeah," Woodruff said, staring at the moonlit water. "I know it's the phosphorus in the air, isn't it? In the incandescent glow you see things."

"So they say."

"I once saw a dog in a wild leap against the sky. There it was, floating by."

"Your dog?"

"No, my father's. He was very fond of that dog, but he died, and I didn't want the dog. Had to get rid of it."

"I see."

"I'm sure that dog is happier out there in that light, leaping over the moon, than he would have been if I had kept him," and he laughed. "Why the Samovar, No.1?"

"I don't know. Maybe . . . well, yes, we had a party there two nights before this sailing."

"There you are," Woodruff said, "God knows what's sailing around for us out there," and he went along the deck.

But it hadn't been a good party. Leo Cawthra, who'd been taking his leave in Montreal with a plump adoring little blonde, had joined him and Julia for an evening. The old Russian woman who ran the Samovar and called him "her boy" had a table for them, and when it got so late that even the orchestra had gone home, she kept one sleepy piano-player on the job. Julia didn't want to go home and she was in an unpredictable mood. She had been drinking and laughing. They were all singing. Then Julia took off her shoes, got up on the table, and, holding her skirts high, began to dance. Her shoulder-length black hair whirled around her face, her brown eyes were shining. He heard Cawthra's blonde whisper, "My God, isn't she awful?" Julia fell off the table and into his arms and started to cry. He had thought he knew Julia, a girl who hated ambiguities, and it had been strange to find her trying to hold him back from going to sea. She'd kept telling him he wasn't himself, it might be a long time before he became himself, he should turn back, he should stay ashore. But what mystified him, as he turned away from the rail and that incandescent sky and went back to his cabin, was why a table with one empty chair?

Yet he slept well, and in the sunlit morning the sea was unbelievably calm, and coming along the upper deck he saw Horler join two stokers, who were taking it easy.

Between the stokers and the seamen there was a natural rivalry. The stokers, who had their own mess, pretended to have an understanding that when anything really important happened the seamen called on them. One of the stokers, heavy and quite bald, mopped his head with a brown handkerchief, and the other, short and fair-haired, with a high intellectual forehead, stood there daydreaming. They wore blue discolored pants and blue shirts; the oil of the engine room had eaten into the skin on their arms. Horler, catching Ira Groome's eye, winked at him, then took a four-foot length of rope out of his pocket. "Either one of you got two bits?" he asked the stokers.

"What for?"

"Two bits no stoker can do the little trick I'll show you."

"Anything a fucking deck hand can do, I can do."

"Okay, stoker," the bosun said, laying the rope flat on the deck. In a couple of deft movements, he made several links in it, using only one hand, then suddenly lifted the rope neatly from the deck. "There you are — tied in a knot. Okay, stoker, let's see you do it."

"Watch me," the stoker with the high forehead said laconically. He tried to make exactly the same movements with the rope, and after each motion he lifted the rope eagerly, but the knot was not in it. Getting down on one knee, his face grim, he made the movements very slowly and stubbornly, then, mystified, looked for a long time at the rope. "I did the same fucking thing you did," he muttered.

"Just too fucking complicated for a stoker," the bosun said.

"Here. Let me see the fucking thing," said the other stoker. Starting slowly, then changing his style, he tried to make the final links rapidly. The still unknotted rope fascinated him. "It's so simple, a child could do it," he whispered.

"But not a fucking stoker."

"Horler, you're a magician," Groome said. As he stood wondering why the word "fucking" lost all its meaning on a ship and was never applied to anything that had to do with a woman, a cry came from the lookout: "Boat on red 20, sir." He went to the rail, where he was quickly joined by Horler, tucking the rope in his pocket as they watched a small boat come drifting aimlessly into the path of the corvette.

"Looks like survivors from some ship in the convoy ahead," he said to Horler. "We may get a signal to pick them up." If there had been survivors from a ship sunk in their own convoy, the corvette wouldn't have stopped to do any rescue work; you don't turn back for anything when ships are under attack. But everything was in good order; as the small boat drifted toward them with a figure in it waving frantically, the signal came from the destroyer ordering them to investigate. They moved in closer until the boat was alongside. In the boat a little black-bearded man in a black sweater threw out his arms in joy. Behind him they could see a big-shouldered red-haired fellow, in a frozen crouch with his arms around a woman who huddled against him. This big man wore only a thin, V-necked light pullover sweater; he seemed to be trying to warm the woman, wrapping her in a man's gray topcoat, which was over another mauve-colored coat; you could see the mauve strip around her knees as she tried to move, looking up mutely at the row of faces along the rail. A line was thrown. She made a feeble attempt to grab at it and missed; but the little fellow grabbed it, and shouted and waved enthusiastically even while the Jacob's ladder was lowered.

"All right, come on up," Horler called.

But the little man, still holding the rope, did not come clambering up the ladder; instead he nodded to the woman who spoke to the big man who still held on to her, seemingly frozen into that one protective position. She shook her head frantically. She remained locked in his rigid arms. The little fellow, grabbing at the big man's arm, pulled him away from the girl, then tried to put the rope in the big fellow's hand. It was no good. He couldn't hold the rope. Rolling onto his knees, the big man worked his arms, trying to get some circulation, then, grabbing the rope, he tugged at it, and slowly hoisted himself to his feet.

"Can you make it?" Horler shouted.

"He'll make it," the little man shouted.

They were both giving the big fellow a slow push toward the ladder, pushing him up, and he came very slowly, helped every so often by the roll of the ship, and then they saw that his face was blue. That blue face with the red stubble of beard! At each rung in the ladder he had to rest, closing his eyes. He lurched, he would have fallen, but a seaman's hand came down and grabbed him. Other hands reached for his shoulders. Up he came over the rail. And he had blazing, frantic blue eyes that shifted around trying to take in where he was as he came down on the deck like a heavy, wet sack. Even then he managed to roll so that he could lie and watch the rail. With his wild, staring eyes he seemed to be pulling the girl up the ladder, pulling till her matted wet blonde head appeared and the seamen pulled her aboard. And when she came safely over the side, the shivering, prostrate big fellow, waving his hand feebly, fell back and closed his eyes. She keeled over, her mouth wide open, and lay blacked out on the deck beside him. The bearded little man came up the ladder and stood there grinning, while the bosun threw a blanket around the girl. The shivering big man in the ridiculous light sweater was trying to talk to the girl. His lips hardly moved. A guttural sound came from his throat. Then a whisper. And only when he heard them saying that the boat could not be left afloat, since it might take another ship off its course investigating, did he raise his head. Only when they had fired a few shots into the boat did he take his eyes off the girl. He tried to stagger to his feet and to take a last look at the boat, but he couldn't make it.

From the bridge the Captain called, "Have the woman taken to the sick bay, No. 1. Try and look after her. Take the men below." And he said, "Where's the sick-bay attendant?" But Mason, the attendant, had already joined them. He had been sleeping in his hammock, which was on the port side of the communications mess, the place for cooks and stewards. Mason was in his blue shirt covered with an old faded orange pullover. In civilian life, he had been an ambulance attendant. He had picked up a lot of medical information riding with the dying and the injured while doctors worked on them. He was a very dignified boy and no one knew how he managed to have this air, for he was just the tiffy, an innocent blue-eyed tiffy, but a strange one, for a seaman had caught him on his knees praying in the mess deck, and he had stood up smiling. In a training exercise at Pictou, when the Captain had given the order to abandon ship, everyone had gone over the side but Mason. The Captain roared at him. "Abandon ship, do you hear?" Mason came to attention, jumped over the side, and was drowning. They hauled him in. He couldn't swim. The Captain said, "Why didn't you say you couldn't swim when I shouted at you?" And Mason said simply, "You didn't ask me, sir."

Two of the hands, Boseley and Jakes, had picked up the girl and were carrying her to the sick bay, and Groome followed with Mason. The sick bay was a small, bright room with a bunk, a chair, a chest, a basin. Some old magazines were on the chest. "Don't put her on the bed till you get those wet clothes off her," he said.

"Put her where, sir?"

"Well, there on the deck," he said. They put her down on her side, and then as Boseley began pulling the coat off her, she was rolled onto her stomach, then onto her back. Her face was ashen, her mouth hanging open. He didn't like the interested expression on Boseley's face. "All right," he said, "Mason can look after this now," and Boseley and Jakes left. "Let's get these things off her, Mason," he said. Mason, who had his ammonia bottle, kept drawing the bottle under her nostrils, but she didn't stir. Then Mason got the wet dress off her. Taking it from Mason he looked at it and dropped it on the floor. "For God's sake, look at this," Mason said. "Long johns, ten sizes too big. Where would she get them, sir?" And he knelt down, helping Mason peel the heavy, wet wool from her waist and legs.

She gagged, half coughed. The sudden closing of her mouth

startled him. Mason had taken the towel to her, drying her quickly as she lay naked with her wet clothes in a little pile on the deck, the pile a wet patch on the deck. Then he saw that her pubic hair was black, though her head was blonde. And this suddenly moved him, seemed to give her a life of her own, and he said to Mason, "Give me the towel," for Mason had not touched her matted wet blonde hair. He began to dry the hair gently, letting the water soak into the towel, then rubbing her scalp, rubbing and wanting her eyes to open, noticing that the roots of her hair were dark. In her cheeks there was now some color. She had long legs, a very slender body, and small firm breasts that he noticed now she was no longer wet and cold. Wrapping the blanket around her they put her on the bunk, and while Mason tucked her in he rubbed her wrists and hands, believing she was conscious. When he was pushing back the hair from her forehead, she clutched his hand. Her eyes had not opened, not as far as he could tell, and as he looked at her long, strong fingers, she shivered. He couldn't free his hand as he bent over her, trying to catch her broken words.

"So they couldn't get us, eh? You're out of your mind. They're not going to get us, eh?" The whispered words came too quickly. Her lips kept moving, forming words, though none came; then he was sure he heard her whisper, "He's full of shit." She began to breathe more naturally. She was quiet; they thought she was asleep, and maybe she was, but her grip on his hand tightened, one eye opened, and in half-dreaming agitation she whispered, " . . . mustn't get away . . . don't let him . . . "

"Miss . . . " he said. "Miss . . . " But she seemed to be truly asleep, so he looked at her face with the high cheekbones — a face with an elegant bone structure. "I think she's asleep," he said.

"What was all that about, No. 1?" Mason asked.

"Strange stuff, eh?"

"Yeah, just dreamy stuff, I guess," Mason said. "I've heard stuff like that a hundred times. I pay no attention to it. She's all right now."

"Well, we can leave her here, I suppose."

"What if we need this place?"

"Out she goes." And he looked at her, and she had her head turned to one side. She must have heard them. Her eyes

67

flickered, though they did not open. She reached for the security of his hand. Nothing was said for a few moments.

"Thank you," she said drowsily. "It's wonderful to feel warm again."

"We'll get you some hot soup."

"Thanks."

"Miss . . . "

"Yeah?"

"What happened?"

"The explosion," she whispered, her mouth trembling. "The boat was lowered, it tipped, then there was only the little man from the ship and Jethroe."

"Who are you? What's your name, Miss?"

"Gina Bixby. We're meeting my father in London."

"What does he do in London?"

"An investment banker . . . Mr. Chone is with him." She turned away, drowsy and ready for a real sleep.

"Get her some clothes. Some sea boots, too," he said to Mason, who was picking up the wet clothes. "Give her a life belt, tell her to wear it and warn her about the action stations. But first we'd better look at that big redhead," and he led the way to the mess deck.

NINE ~~~~~~

"What do you make of her, Mason? How old?"

"Twenty-four or twenty-five. Always had it pretty soft."

"You can tell?"

"By her hands and feet."

"Come on, Mason. Fifty years ago, maybe."

"Okay, fifty years ago. But look, No. 1, a woman on ship
. . . Won't some of the hands say it's bad luck?"

"Not our hands, Mason. Not a sea-dog among them. They
all really belong somewhere else. Plumbers, taxi drivers, door-to-
door salesmen."

They were at the watertight door to the seamen's mess deck,

then passing the refrigerator which must have been just opened, for there was a smell of food kept too long. The whole mess deck had the stale family odor of thirty men living carelessly and intimately, eating and sleeping together in a ship-wide place like a cellar going back deep to the watertight door at the bow; a cluttered-up cellar in someone's old house with hammocks slung from bars on the ceiling. As the ship swayed he had to duck, or have his head caught by a hammock. Naked bulbs above the swaying hammocks made them look like twisted vines in a jungle. In these hammocks some men were still asleep. Bits of gear were sticking out of lockers; dishes on cupboards. On the long seat with its leather cushion sat the little bright-eyed, black-bearded survivor, wrapped in blankets and eating a bowl of hot soup. He grinned at Ira Groome.

On one of the three long tables lay the big red-haired man, covered with many blankets. Two seamen bent over him. One, Horler, kept patting his head, whispering. The other, leading seaman Henderson, saw the sick-bay attendant. "Well, here's the tiffy," he said. "Maybe he can do something," and Mason joined them with his ammonia bottle.

"This guy is in pretty bad shape, No.1!" Horler said.

"Shivering like that. At least he's conscious."

"Yeah, but in a funny kind of way, sir. His eyes keep opening, then closing, and he mumbles and tries to grin and goes into some kind of a shivering convulsion. Never saw a man so goddamned cold, sir."

"Can't you warm him?"

"Look at him."

"All those blankets."

"Seems to be in some kind of a shock," Mason said. "Maybe we should get a bit of morphine into him. Can you get into shock from the cold? Do you know anything about morphine, No. 1?"

"Not a damned thing," and then he turned to the happy-eyed merchant seaman who had finished his bowl of soup.

"Why is he in this shape?" he asked.

"The girl got his clothes. He gave them to her," the merchant seaman said in a broad Yorkshire accent. "You see, sir, he takes off his bloody coat and puts it around her own coat, and when she goes numb again, so help me, Jesus, he takes off his pants, so he can take off those bloody long heavy drawers he had on for the occasion, and he puts them on her. Never saw anything like it, and he's in that cold last night, soaking wet too in that light suit-coat."

"His name is Chone?"

"Yes sir. Jethroe Chone."

"Mr. Chone," he called, bending over him.

Under the light from the naked bulb, Jethroe Chone, with his nose and high cheekbones, looked like an Indian. But he had reddish stubble on his face, and red hair. A shivering red-bearded Indian whose teeth wouldn't stop chattering, and whose staring blue eyes were as hard and cold as the sea. Bending over Chone he felt that the man, whose eyes were on him, was seeing something very vividly, and couldn't turn away from it. "Mr. Chone . . . ," he said. And then on a hunch he added, "Miss Bixby is all right. She's fine." He repeated this, and repeated it till the blue eyes focused on him. A few words came, but they were so slurred by the rattle of his teeth they were hard to follow. "Sure. Sure. They try and they'll try again. And it won't do the sons of bitches any good at all . . . " Then his whole body shivered and he tried to control his jaw.

"Nothing to do but leave him," Mason said, "or pack him with hot-water bottles."

"Naked under those blankets, Mason?"

"Right, No. 1."

"What about a man . . . " he began, then hesitated. "A man could get under those blankets, someone warm and naked, hugging him tight," and he waited, hands on hips.

No one said anything. He could see himself doing it; holding the shivering man in his arms, warming him, till he became a man again. The thing was in his face for them to see, and the signalman, that sea lawyer, believing their No. 1 was going to take off his clothes in the mess deck, their mess deck, their home, frowned and looked offended. And the look on the signalman's face told the others they ought to be offended, too, so they were, and waited awkwardly. Horler was the most embarrassed. But there was questioning good will in Horler's eyes, a loyalty, too . . . and he shouted, "Maybe he's got the right idea. I'll be damned if I can't warm the poor bastard," and he began to pull off his clothes. No one said a word, not even when he was

71

naked. "Okay, men," he said, then, getting under the blankets with Chone, he wrapped his arms tight around him. "Pile the blankets on."

The bearded Yorkshireman got up wrapped in his blanket and came to the table to watch with the others. Little was said. Minutes passed. "Jesus," Horler said. "I'm getting tired of this." Yet he held on to Chone. Finally Chone's teeth stopped chattering. Everyone leaned closer, fascinated, for he now had his jaw under control. Gradually his breathing became easier, the pale blue eyes opened, shifted around from face to face, to the swinging hammocks, showing apprehension and suspicion; and then, as he got the hang of things, his hand came up from under the blanket, reaching for Horler's head, a big hand with an enlarged knuckle, a broken knuckle, and he moved the hand along Horler's face as if he wanted to remember its shape even if he were never to see it. "Thanks," he whispered.

"What the hell is this?" Horler shouted. Reddening with embarrassment, he threw off the blankets and bounded on to the deck. Everyone laughed. Everyone was happy. "That was a great idea, No. 1," Horler said. "Wasn't it, Mason?"

"I'm the one who should have thought of it," Mason said.

On the bridge, the Captain turned to Jackson, the navigator, whose face in the sunlight really was the color of mahogany, then stepped into the radar cabin, and out again. There against the backdrop of the blue sunlit sea he looked so magnificently and squarely naval: square-faced, square-chinned, a figure of solid naval authority in repose. Yet he was just happy to be away from home, and would be happier still if he thought the war could go on for years and keep him away. He had had a bad time at home. He had been a small-town high-school history teacher married to a beautiful girl who had looked up to him. He had got transferred to the city. In the city, she had met some advertising men who showed her that she was beautiful and got her some modelling jobs. She learned that beautiful women need money and attention, more money than her husband, a high-school teacher, could give her, and she nagged at him till she persuaded him that all the money was in selling. She had acquired a friend who was a big insurance salesman; so the Captain, her husband, had quit teaching to sell life insurance, and he hated it. He started drinking. "Never, never marry a beautiful woman unless you have a lot of money," he had once said. But in the war he found freedom and respect in the rules and regulations. If the war could go on for years, then his wife, in her season, would lose some of her beauty; he could then go home. Or if he got rich by some miracle, he could go home.

"Well, what's the situation, No.1?" he said. "Who are those people?"

"The merchant seaman is in great shape," he said. "The girl is all right now, sir, so is the big fellow. Seems they sailed from Boston. Bixby is the girl's name. Chone, the man, works with her father. Financial men evidently. Investment bankers . . . business in London, now."

"Hmm. Money men," the Captain said. "Bixby is the name, you say?"

"Bixby, sir."

"Wall Street, or London?"

"Well, they're American, sir."

"Well, No. 1, you never know what you run into, or what you may pick up at sea. You may even end up with a friend at court," and he had a flinty, hard, cynical smile. "Might as well sound out that fellow, what's his name — Chone?" and he turned away. The navigator, coming out of the radar cabin, stood for a moment looking across the water at distant ships in their lanes, then turned and smiled. And against his mahogany face his long upper lip, now that he was smiling, really looked like a scimitar.

TEN ≈≈≈≈≈≈≈≈≈≈≈≈≈≈≈≈≈≈≈≈≈≈≈≈

In the morning, coming up from the wardroom, he heard voices to the port side, Mason and Boseley: "Tell me more, Mason. Come on, you put her to bed."

"I told you, Bo, she's a nice girl. Nice to talk to, too." And Boseley said, "I know that. I talked to her myself. I said, 'I'm the one that carried you into the sick bay,' and you know Mason, I think she gave me the eye. But she'd be expensive, I can tell when they're expensive." Mason was laughing.

"A guy like you could never get near her, Bo." And Boseley said, "In my taxi I get near women all the time. A guy hacking for a living gets to know how to make it."

74

"Like how, Bo?" So Boseley said profoundly, "Do things for them. I carry their parcels from the cab and I say very little, but my eyes shriek, 'My God it must be wonderful to be with a woman like you,' then . . . "

"So then, Bo?"

"Then they invite me in for a coffee and I'm really in. The thing is, how much would that lady cost me?" Then they moved along.

He saw her on the flats by the sick bay where the silhouettes of the different U-boats were pasted on the bulkhead. "Hello," she called, and the seaman's blue sweater she wore actually seemed to fit her good square shoulders and hang loosely. The blonde hair was combed now; it hung to her shoulders; and she had on a seaman's blue serge pants, and sea boots, and a lifebelt. These things on her looked as if she had chosen them deliberately. Yet her smile couldn't hide that she was still half-stunned and nervous.

"I don't know," she said. "I'm still in a kind of daze. My mind wants to go blank . . . if I try and remember. I thought my foot had been frozen, it kept paining. Yet I know I'm all right. How's Mr. Chone?"

"Thawed out. He's all right."

"I don't know your name, Lieutenant."

"Groome. Ira Groome."

"Ira Groome. Well, thank you for looking after me. I'm Gina Bixby," and she put out her hand as if she were welcoming him into her own house. "You were very gentle with me, Mr. Groome," she said. "When you were putting the blankets around me I saw your face . . . I don't know, I felt very safe and warm and then full of sleep," and she looked around. "Should I stay here . . . in this area?"

"Oh no. Feel free to go along the deck, Miss Bixby."

"No one will mind?"

"No one," he said, so she came along the deck with him. "Before this naval thing, what did you do for a living, Mr. Groome?" she asked, and he said he was in archeology, attached to a museum, and had been on a dig in the Yucatan.

"Oh, lots of pre-Columbian art, right under your eyes," she said.

"Well, it's there to wonder about."

"I like it. My father has three fine pieces."

75

"In that case, you probably know more about it than I do. What do you do ashore, Miss Bixby?"

"I had a job with a publisher in Boston. Some other Smith girls were there. Smith girls are all over the place in the east. I was only doing secretarial work, but I was supposed to get into the editorial side. That's why I took that job. A foothold. I wanted to write."

"What kind of writing."

"Sports."

"Really, Miss Bixby?"

"Yes. Really. I wrote verse too. They didn't like my verse."

"Who didn't like it?"

"The school editors at Smith. They wouldn't print my sports pieces either. I didn't expect them to."

"I don't know any women sports writers."

"That's all right. Just wait a little."

"Were you a girl athlete at college? A pole-vaulter or something?"

"Gosh, no. Tennis or skiing. Outside of that —" she laughed suddenly. "Don't worry. I know the sports world. Very manly, very funny. Very corrupt. All the high priests! The only national religion, you know. There's a kind of rough poetry in it. I got to know all about it hanging around my father."

"Your father?" he said, surprised. The investment banker now in London? Then he saw Mr. Chone coming along the deck in a thick gray sweater, the sun on his reddish hair, and he looked like a big powerful man though he couldn't have been more than five foot ten. But he was very heavy-chested, and strong through the shoulders, with big powerful hands. And somehow he did not look out of place there on the deck. Solemn-faced, he stared at Miss Bixby, and as he came closer and saw she was at ease he grinned broadly.

"You'll want to talk to Mr. Chone," Ira Groome said. "I'll be on my way." But he couldn't resist looking back. He remembered how she had whispered, "Don't let him get away," sounding like a policewoman. Now Chone, full of relief, had his hands out to her. He was questioning her rapidly. She answered and almost at once they fell into a casual ease as if they had been through other bad experiences together. What goes on between those two, he wondered. And minutes later when he saw them at the port rail watching the water he looked up at the bridge and saw that the Captain was watching them, so he approached them himself.

"Well, Mr. Chone," he said, "you look as fit as a fiddle, doesn't he, Miss Bixby?"

"Mr. Chone is a hard man to put down," she said.

"Sleep is a wonderful thing, isn't it ?" Chone said, smiling faintly. "I'm not superstitious, sir, but I woke up once. All the muttering and whispering and snoring. I thought I was in the pit. I didn't know what it was. I'm in hell, I thought, then I figured out it was the men sleeping in hammocks around me."

He sounded like some kind of a public figure. His words came a little too slowly, a little too carefully, as if he had been taught to avoid slurring his speech. And he hadn't shaved; he was keeping his red beard. He might have been about thirty-five. Yet, around his eyes he looked older. He had shrewdly watchful blue eyes. Even when he laughed, the expression in his eyes didn't change.

"Well, you're lucky, Mr. Chone," he said. "Maybe you'll bring us luck all the way."

"Are we going to need such luck?" she asked anxiously. "I'm as jumpy as a cat."

"Gina, Gina, we're warm, we're safe, aren't we? We made it," he said.

"No more U-boats, Jethroe?"

"We're the hunters now, Gina. It's an escort vessel."

"Whatever that means."

"It's like being given a lift by a police car," he joked. "Isn't that right, sir?" Before he could reply the Captain called from the bridge, "Mr. Chone . . . "

"Yes, sir?"

"Feel free to come up on the bridge, Mr. Chone."

"Thank you, sir," Chone called, then turning to Miss Bixby, "Very nice of him, eh?" he said solemnly. "Well, I'd better go up on that bridge." His approach to the bridge was dignified and impressive. He climbed the ladder slowly, said a few words to the Captain, and they saw him shake hands with the navigator. Left to himself, then, he was a big, solid, impressive figure looking over the water.

"Well, I'll be damned," Miss Bixby said softly. "How in hell did he get up there?"

77

"He's impressive, I suppose," he said.

"You think so?"

"Well, the way he looked after you . . . and got himself in that condition. I never saw a man so cold."

"Well, yes, it's true, I suppose," and she shrugged.

"He couldn't have done much more."

"I don't suppose he could have."

"Even gave you that long underwear of his."

"It's a fact."

"I don't know," he said, astonished by her lack of appreciation.

"He was quite heroic, eh?"

"He certainly was, Miss Bixby."

"Oh, I agree."

"You're very lucky to have someone so concerned about you."

"You bet," and again she shrugged. "Jethroe Chone's always there."

"Doing things like that? "

"This and that. It's the way it goes."

"I'm sorry, Miss Bixby. It really isn't my business, but . . . "

"But what?"

"I mean, I can't see a banker doing that kind of stuff, and as you say, being always there to do it."

"No," she said and hesitated, then touched him on the arm. "Well, to tell you the truth, and I suppose I should since I don't know what'll happen now, my father's not a banker."

"But in the sick bay you said . . . "

"That's a kind of family joke. My father, as a joke, describes himself as an investment banker. You see, he was a mining engineer who got in with some prospectors and he struck it very rich . . . iron ore on the north shore of Lake Superior. Now he's able to do the things that always fascinated him. He's a gambler. A professional gambler, a big one. It's all he does . . . and Chone? I just told him you must have the impression he's a financial man."

"What did he say?"

"Just laughed."

"What is he then?"

"My father's bodyguard."

"Well, I'll be damned," he said, and turned to look at Chone up on the bridge, outlined against the sky. "Hmmm," he said, "I must say your father's man doesn't look out of place on that bridge. A well-spoken man, too. Does your father need a bodyguard?"

"Where there's big gambling there's big hoods."

"Well, he fooled me."

"No one takes him for a mug now," she said, shrugging. "My father took quite an interest in him."

Chone, on the bridge, saw them watching him, and he bowed.

"Look at him," she said, taking an amused tone. "Well, big and all as he looks up there, he's just a pocket edition of my father. If you saw him by my father in a New York restaurant, you'd get the point."

"Yes, I think I would."

"Well, now that everyone's in his right place ... "

"Back to the sick bay for you, Miss Bixby, is that it?"

"Might as well," she said, "I'll catch up on some of those old magazines."

"Why not?" he said, and as she turned away he put his hand on her arm, indicating he would go along the deck with her. But at the feel of her, those other parts he had inadvertently touched, breast, belly, inner thigh, when she had been naked and cold as a corpse and he had rolled her in the blankets, now seemed warmly alive. The effect on him was so quick and surprising he hardly heard her saying, " ... and after the war you'll go back to it."

"Back ... ?"

"To archeology."

"Oh. Well, I don't know. At least not with the same crowd."

"Why not?"

"I was fired, Miss Bixby."

"You fired?"

"I was," and he grinned, "I had a fight with my boss, the professor."

"Not a real fight?"

"Nothing you could sell tickets to," he said. "A big bald man with a beard, we'd been drinking and it got insulting, so I nailed him on the jaw. So I came home and joined the navy."

"And that's archeology?"

"No, just two archeologists. Two different views of things."
They were stopped by the sick bay and she looked so interested
that he said, "It's not much of a story, but at least it's what
happened." He told her about how four of them, near an ancient
Mayan village on the edge of a Yucatan jungle, had been working on a great mound covered with vegetation. It had been one
of those low pyramids, maybe two thousand years old. As for
what happened, well, it wasn't the jungle. It was really because
of the Mayan village so close to the Mayans, every bit as Mayan
as they had been two thousand years ago, with their strange pa-
tience and dignity, going through religious rituals whose meaning they had forgotten, just as whatever had made them great
had been long since forgotten. Yet they were there. And one
night, maybe the moon did it to him, it struck him that he was
working in a boneyard, a graveyard, and the skulls they dug up,
the ruins, the sacrificial stones, told nothing about the life that
had been lived there and the way those people felt about life and
each other. That night he longed to see a ghost, any ghost. He
was there digging in their graveyard, and yet living people, the
same people, were there in the village with all their ancestral life
buried in their memory.

Well, he had turned to them; got to know an eighteen-year-
old girl whose black hair fell to her waist. This girl had a simple
warmth and great dignity. He had some Spanish and she could
speak Spanish. They spent hours together. His professor boss
told him he was neglecting the work and drinking too much.
Maybe it was true. Yet he couldn't get enough of that girl; the
spirit, the feeling in her ancient people, had shaped those stones,
those altars, thousands of years ago. When he held her in his
arms she seemed to be telling him lovely things about her people. When she held him close he was in touch with all her dead.
They were alive in her. Even their stones were alive. It was a
strange, terribly heightened feeling of enchantment, and he
would be saying to himself, "Come on, Marina, remember one
way or another, come on, remember. Remember."

Anyway, Professor Ball asked him to have a drink. They
drank. The professor, needling him, said. "So you have to know
about her ancient people, eh? Well, maybe monuments and
tombs tell us nothing. Their garbage does. If you want to know
about people study their garbage."

"Standing up, I said, 'You're dead, Dr. Ball. I smell the garbage,' and I walked away. The professor screamed, 'Come back here,' and came at me, slapping and clawing, and I clipped him. And here I am, Miss Bixby."

"What about the girl?"

"What about her?"

"Did you get any ancient wisdom out of her?"

"Something."

"You did? About what?"

"How they used to look at the world; cruel and senseless, a nightmare, always was, and always will be, and all we can do is make something beautiful out of the nightmare."

"That's a lot to get. It certainly was," and she seemed astonished. Then, after a moment's silence, she changed. She looked unhappy. "And there's truth in it, isn't there? Such a terrible truth, as I should know," and then in a wondering tone, "You got this out of that little girl, just being with her. She must have wondered if you came from over the water just to get in touch with her. How fascinating," and she drew back, looking full at him as if he had become someone else, then was silent. He didn't know what to say to her. He hadn't been trying to fascinate her, he had only been trying to keep her interested. "It wasn't like that with us," he said. "She never asked where I came from."

"But how beautiful for her," she said softly. "Or for any woman. She was the story. Gentle and loving and all as she may have been, you may be sure she knew she was the whole story for you. Everything, as you say, was in her . . . for a man like you, and she knew it."

"A man like me," he said. "I was on my way." Then they were at the door to the sick bay, where he waited awkwardly while she reflected and finally smiled to herself. "Yes," she said. "I'll bet that girl really must have wondered where you came from." And then very gravely, "Where did you come from, Ira Groome?"

"You're a funny girl," he said.

"These are funny times . . . for me," she said.

"The bridge," he said suddenly, as Chone came into his mind. "Chone, up on that bridge, the bodyguard."

"The Captain invited him."

"Yeah, after I told him he was an important investment

banker," and he tried to laugh. "Excuse me, Miss Bixby." As he went along the deck he thought of how the Captain would sound Chone out, maybe over a drink. Then in his own style he would sneak up on him with apparently irrelevant friendly questions. Bit by bit he would get at Chone's background. The Captain was good at this. What schools had Chone gone to? What was his university? His view of money? What did he think of John Maynard Keynes? And all the time the Captain, enjoying his scholarly perceptions, wouldn't betray his own opinion of Chone.

Though he thought his mind was entirely on Chone, he turned suddenly and looked back. She still stood at the sick-bay entrance, and she was watching him intently with an expression he could not fathom.

∼∼∼∼∼∼∼∼∼∼∼∼∼∼∼∼∼∼∼∼∼∼∼∼

ELEVEN

With the sea calm in the afternoon sunlight and monotony settling over the whole ship, he was on the bridge with the glasses to his eyes, watching one tanker out there in the roughly drawn lane of ships. This ship was falling back. He wasn't sure yet that it was a straggler. "One of those ships doesn't seem to be in place," he said to the Captain, who was at the voice tube. "Take a look, sir." And the Captain looked and said finally, "May be a little engine trouble. It may have moved up shortly. We'll give it a little time."

And then he said suddenly, "There's a sight for you. There just off the port bow." A dead man in a pair of shorts, held by a lifebelt in a sitting position, sailed along below the water line as if on an invisible chair.

"A little sign of some action ahead, sir," he said.

"Not if the Commodore can avoid it," the Captain said as the sound of laughter came from men sprawled out under the gun turret, then the sound of someone running down a ladder, then of men singing softly.

"There's a virgin up in Newfie so they say, there's a virgin so they say, she'll be six months old today . . . " and the sea was becoming slate gray with sun-made streaks of quicksilver sliding and flowing over the slate in the sea's swell. To starboard some porpoises wiggled and played in the water. Sea pigs. Wonderful, friendly, and frolicsome. Did they really like ships and men, he wondered, or was it, as some people said, that they liked insects. Always a cluster of insects at the bow or the stern. Porpoises and men! They roll and play in the quicksilvered gray sea while sitting men float by in their underwear.

The convoy's destroyer had begun to flash the execution signal to alter course twenty degrees. It was part of the game, the countermove against U-boats waiting in a pack at a certain rendezvous. And now as the ships wheeled in their courses it was like watching a great clumsy mechanical ballet.

"The choreography of the sea war," he said to the Captain, who nodded appreciatively. As the ships in their roughly drawn lanes wheeled, the lanes were broken; now they were just a jumble of dirty gray blotches moving against the backdrop of the clear blue sky, then the jumble of objects was gradually arranged into a new pattern at new angles — a controlled and organized pattern again.

He saw Miss Bixby going slowly toward the stern, stopping sometimes to grip the rail, then withdrawing her hand, then touching the rail again, then running her hand along it as if bent on getting used to one of the things around her. He saw Boseley stand up on the rear gun turret to take a long look at her. Then a P.O. appeared at her side; in a few seconds she had put him at ease; she was questioning him. Soon he was pointing to the quarterdeck and talking volubly, and the odds were he was telling her why sailors salute the quarterdeck. Then he noticed that she was in her bare feet. While he was watching her feet he grew troubled. Those mumbled words of hers when she had been half-conscious in the sick bay: words that would have made any intelligence officer prick up his ears suspiciously: "They missed again. Keep on missing. They keep on missing," then her derisive mumbling, "Oh, yeah, and he's full of shit." Who were "they"? he wondered.

And Jethroe Chone. The same thing with him. Chone had whispered so incoherently, "This was their best shot and they missed. They don't know they're out of it." Who were they? Now the P.O. had left her and she was coming along the deck. Leaving the bridge, he found her in the flats by the sick bay.

"Hello, Miss Bixby," he said. "Getting along all right?"

"I'm fine. Thank you."

"And Mr. Chone?"

"The banker?" she said sardonically. "Maybe he's in your Captain's cabin enjoying a drink — waiting for the Captain."

"You may be right," he said, then, standing at the rail with the sea sparkling in the sunlight, he said,

"By the way, there was something I meant to ask you, Miss Bixby."

"What was that?"

"Something you said in the sick bay. Who are 'they' "?

"They?"

"Sounded as if you and Chone believed someone knew you were on that ship."

"And the ship went down?"

"It certainly went down."

"I see," she said. The silence was too prolonged. It was provoking. Finally she said, "They, eh? No, not enemy agents, Lieutenant. Marty Rosso's crowd."

"Marty Rosso?"

"Don't you ever read the sports pages in the papers ?"

"Now and then."

"Anyway, until a few weeks ago you wouldn't have seen Rosso's name in the papers," she said, shrugging. "No one ever printed anything about Rosso. Now he's on the front page. In New York, anyway. The District Attorney is holding an enquiry. Arena owners all across the country are parading in. Fixing the fights. Fixing everything in the world. You see, Marty Rosso owns about thirty fighters. You don't fight in the Garden unless you're a Rosso fighter, and, of course, there's a big gambling tie-up right across the country. Rosso's mixed up with race tracks too. A vicious gambler with powerful connections, and you know, until the last few weeks his name never even appeared in the papers. Now his head may be on the chopping block, so they say."

"And this Rosso is after Chone?"

"Well, yes . . ."

"And Chone thinks . . . Well, for God's sake," and he started to laugh. "Is Chone crazy?"

"Not at all. Why?"

"This is a little wild."

"How so?"

"Does he think the war is fixed?" and he laughed again.

"Don't laugh. He's not crazy. He may know more about the war than you and I do. But of course he doesn't believe anything the politicians or the generals say about it."

"Wait a minute — please. This Rosso crowd. What did Chone do?"

"Nothing. It's me."

"You?"

The sun sparkled on the blue quiet sea and her eyes were on some spot far away on the horizon where the sky and the sea met in a thin mist. Finally she said, "Someone here should know something about me — in case anything happens, and I'd like it to be you. It feels right that it should be you, okay?" In her even, modulated tone she began to talk about herself. That cultivated tone in the bright monotony of the afternoon made him feel he was getting only the facts.

He would have to know something about her life. There had been a side to it, even when she had been at Smith, that had taken her away from the girls in her campus house. She had liked college, she had loved the intellectual stimulation. She had always been half in love with some English professor, dating some boy from Amherst, or looking for some man from Yale who loved poetry. On weekends, writing her essays on Eliot and Auden, she would grow restless and start dreaming of the lawless excitement of her father's world. She started to go into New York on weekends. She had the money to do it. In restaurants and clubs she sat around with her father and the sports crowd. And Jethroe Chone was always there, following her father's instructions and looking after her. If some clown got out of line Chone's big hand would tap him on the arm. "All right, buster, that'll do." He used to make her feel that she was the family jewel, or a princess out slumming, even when she had a girlfriend from Smith with her.

She went on to say that her father had taken her to Europe, and in Paris they had gone to one of those small clubs that had fight cards. Her father had been impressed by a good-looking boy named Robert Riopelle, a middleweight, a lonely-looking boy, a kid, with all the great natural talents. The French boy had a strangely moving, noble character. The kid took a shine to her father, too. Anyway, her father paid Riopelle's way here and set him up with an old manager he trusted, Whitey Unger, and had him fighting out of Montreal where as a French-speaker he had no trouble with the language. There was nothing in it for her father. Well, one thing — the joy of watching the triumph of his judgment. But that was his great joy in things now, and he had the money for it. Whitey Unger got the boy's contract and he got some money to train him and bring him along slowly while he learned the fundamentals, and soon he was the darling of the Montreal crowd. And then within a year Whitey Unger wrote her father that he had sold a piece of Riopelle's contract to Marty Rosso so Riopelle could fight in the Garden.

"Why are you smiling?" she asked.

"You sound just like a sports writer."

"I'm going to be a sports writer. I told you."

"I thought it was to be poetry."

"That'll come too."

"I think it will," he said. "What about Rosso?"

Had he ever been in Lindy's on Broadway? No, well sitting there one night with an Amherst boy and her father's friend, she heard one of the characters say, "Why don't I write about Rosso? Sure someday someone will, the gate will open and I will too, but right now I have a wife and grandchildren." Rosso's hand reached out to all the big arenas across the country, a terrifying influence. So now the District Attorney was holding an enquiry into the betting ring centered in the Garden. Some years ago Rosso had done a five-year stretch for manslaugher, and there had also been a murder charge he had beaten. So no one fooled around with Rosso.

"Excuse me," he said. The little bearded Yorkshireman was coming aimlessly along the deck, looking at loose ends, and he went over to him.

"Not much to do, eh?" he asked. "Well, it's a health cruise for you."

"I'm in good health, sir."

"Only you'd like to be doing something, eh?"

"That's right, sir."

"You're a good seaman, and a good seaman is never out of place," and he gave him a pat on the shoulder.

"Mr. Groome . . . " she said.

"Yes, ma'am."

"Is that a normal attitude with that man — or is it just you?"

"I beg your pardon . . . "

"Never mind. Well, the gambling, the fixed fights." Leaning on the rail, staring into the water, she went on: The big arena owners all knew they were accommodating Rosso, using his fighters. One of these owners, a St. Louis man, a very rich man from the oil business, had a daughter, a friend of hers at Smith, quite an equestrienne. And this rich man appeared at the District Attorney's enquiry and you could tell he found Rosso's friendship fascinating. Imagine! No one would talk, no one knew anything. Were the rich men fascinated, or excited? Or just plain scared to? Well, to go back a little. Whitey Unger had made her father sore as hell cutting Rosso in, but her father could see that Riopelle wanted to fight in the Garden. He knew Riopelle couldn't throw a fight. So Riopelle got to the Garden and won fight after fight, all by knockouts.

"But I could have read this in the newspapers," he said, interrupting her.

"So you could. The facts. I'm giving you the facts."

"But you and Chone?"

"You'll have to let me go on," she said.

A big white cloud drifted across the sun and the water lost its sparkle: it was slate gray, and now it felt colder on deck; and then as the heavy drifting cloud thinned, the sun came out.

"Do you know about the middleweight champion, Gus De-Horla, a Rosso fighter?" she asked. He did? Then he must know about old Jimmie Johnson, who had been champion and had retired. Good. Johnson was the one her father had described as the greatest fighter, pound for pound, who ever lived. In her debutante voice, she was talking to him as if she knew he wouldn't have any real information about the first game.

Well, three years ago Johnson had come out of retirement, she went on, and in six or seven warm-up fights he got back all his old form. The champion, DeHorla, who hadn't had a title fight in two years, had been ordered by the Boxing Commission to lay his title on the line, or give it up. So a fight was arranged. Not with Johnson, of course. DeHorla was giving Riopelle a shot at the title. A big warm-up for his big fight with Johnson, and this fight was to be staged in the Montreal ball park for all those crazy Riopelle fans. She had a girlfriend, Michelle, who had gone to the Sacred Heart Convent before coming to Smith, and who was in Montreal now. So she went with her father to Montreal to see Riopelle fight. Michelle came around to her father's suite at the Ritz and had a Sunday night supper with them.

"Michelle was fascinated by the company my father kept," she said. But a rich man could have any kind of friends, high or low, bright or dumb. Wasn't that true? And there they were, the fight mob, the gamblers and managers and newspapermen, all freeloading on her father; the greatest freeloaders in the world. Everybody well-dressed and carefully polite to the ladies with that heavy, grave, half-formal gallantry which was very funny in a way. Michelle had been fascinated, too, by Jethroe Chone's careful speech. She said Jethroe's eyes made her shiver, and, of course, he was always hovering around them protectively.

"Ready to die for you, isn't he?" she joked.

Whitey Unger looked worried. He took her father aside, then decided he had nothing to say. Later, he tried again. Finally, just before he was leaving, he said out of the corner of his mouth, "Well, there's to be a return match in six months." At the time this meant nothing to her father. He had talked to Riopelle, and the boy, embracing him, told him he would be proud of him. Riopelle loved her father.

Later that night Chone and her father took her and Michelle out "slumming" as Michelle said. They went to an all-night saloon called Slitkin and Slotkin's. Did he know the place? They were the two fantastic clowning characters who insulted their patrons. For intimate friends they had a little bar which remained open long after the restaurant had closed. At a long table at the end of the bar, in a corner, was a small, oily black-haired man with frightened vicious eyes. She remembered how this little man kept beckoning to her father. His name was Coyle. In between fights they humored him, calling him Riopelle's trainer. In those off months he served as Rosso's water boy, running messages. He had been on Rosso's payroll for years, doing all the jobs, according to Chone — working for him, getting the vote out in New York at election time, doing a little knifing or beating job here and there. But Coyle had got sick, he had been in the hospital. Chone said Coyle's kidneys wouldn't work and now he had to use one of those tubes. And, of course, Rosso had discarded him; he was destitute. Her father finally went over to Coyle and sat down. A few minutes later they saw Coyle get up suddenly, look frightened, and hurry out. Her father was white-faced, his eyes murderous. He told them that Coyle had babbled away about "the man" — he never called Rosso anything but "the man" — and how Coyle had to get to "the man" or die of starvation. Then Coyle had let it slip out that Riopelle's fights in the Garden, the great knockouts, had all been fixed. Riopelle didn't know about it. He wasn't in on it. The other boy always took the dive. Coyle had thought her father would know about this. Slumped in the chair, he brooded, then said of Riopelle, "The poor dear sweet honest Christian bastard. How this would break the poor boy's heart. This is a terrible thing."

Back at the hotel, he and Jethroe Chone, putting two and two together, this being their business, asked themselves why Whitey Unger, Riopelle's manager, as if under a deep obligation, had whispered, "There's to be a return match." The bookmakers had made DeHorla a three-to-one favorite. If DeHorla threw the fight, Rosso could make a million. Chone explained the ins and outs of it later, she said, and you should remember what an exotic jungle this world was. Look, if DeHorla lost his title to Riopelle, with Rosso making a million on the deal, then he would not have to fight the great Johnson. The contract would call for a return match between DeHorla and Riopelle. This could take a year. Then DeHorla could get his title back; the Commission would be satisfied. And he could take another year, maybe longer, before fighting Johnson. And by that time Johnson, who was now thirty-six, would be thirty-eight years old. Neat eh? And Riopelle, who was so stupidly honest, and who had such sublime faith in his talent, would never know what had happened.

Her father got to Riopelle the next day, she said. How he did it, she didn't know. But she knew of Riopelle's respect for him. She had read the letters written in French. Her father, who could be a pretty grim, bad customer himself, and wasn't afraid of money, went out at the last minute and bet a hundred thousand on DeHorla. The Montreal bookie had to lay off the bet across the country. Did he know what that meant?

So they were all at the ball park that hot June night for the fight. That crazy French-Canadian crowd loved Riopelle. Anyway, he really was a beauty. And for twelve rounds he had the fight in hand, taking bows between rounds, and the crowd loving him. DeHorla was a heavy puncher. He kept punching hard and sometimes wildly, with Riopelle dancing away, then in the thirteenth round, with DeHorla swinging hard and viciously, always short by inches, Riopelle got hit. Instead of dancing away he had come in, dropped his guard a little, and taken a wild punch. He was knocked out, and there was DeHorla, bewildered and all, still champion, with everybody jumping into the ring.

Her father picked up Riopelle in the dressing room and they got out quickly because the silence in that room had frightened them. In the corridor Whitey Unger caught up with them. Shaking, he whispered to Riopelle, "You crazy son of a bitch. You'd better start running."

Jethroe Chone took her back to the hotel and stayed with her while Riopelle and her father went to an obscure restaurant in the east end. Riopelle had got very little money from Rosso over the last year, it was all owing to him. Her father told Riopelle he would look after him; the money he himself had won would go to Riopelle. As for what happened then, it was all in the newspapers next day. While Riopelle and her father were in a booth in the restaurant, two men, one with a gun, the other with a baseball bat, came at them, and holding the gun on her father, they broke Riopelle's hands with the baseball bat. Not a word was said by these efficient thugs. The job was done, they walked out.

91

After Riopelle had been taken to the hospital to have his poor broken hands treated and bandaged, he was taken to his own place where he sat down and wept. Her father assured him he would have thirty thousand for him; they talked about buying a little bar in Paris where his mother could live with him. A priority on a plane had been wangled for him and a ticket would be there in the morning. The arrangements had all been made; and her father stayed with him until he went to bed. Then her father came hurrying back to her and Chone and insisted she pack at once and get out to the airport. She had never seen him so grim and so alarmed. Chone took her out to the airport where they had to wait three hours before she could get a plane to New York.

The rest of it she got from Jethroe, though this, too, was in all the papers the next day. The New York papers, too. Her father, when he had taken Riopelle home, had assured him he would give him enough money to open a bar in France. Riopelle was to get right out of the country. At the hospital they had given Riopelle pain-killing pills and sleeping tablets, too. In the morning he was found dead, the phials empty of pills. Yet he had ripped the bandages off his hands, as if he had to see the smashed and bleeding hands for the last time; the thing he believed in, that had been corrupted, then smashed forever. In all his fights he had been a nobody. It was in the papers, too, that her father had got in touch with the District Attorney and told him he would appear at the enquiry to talk about Rosso. He arranged for Riopelle's funeral.

She was in New York, staying at the Algonquin, to see about the new job with the publishing firm. She liked the Algonquin because she had read so much about the writers and theater people who had sat drinking in the lounge. The phone call came from Montreal when she was out. She returned the call at night. Her father had left the hotel, they said. Jethroe Chone came walking in on her just when she was going out for her breakfast. He had a room at the Waldorf. He wanted her to move and get a room near him.

"Miss Gina, it's a bad scene," he said. He was quick and gentle and relieved to have found her. First he told her about Riopelle's funeral. There had been one lovely touch. Rosso himself, showing up for the funeral, had stood not ten feet away

92

from her father. Rosso had three henchmen with him who looked like old-fashioned gangsters out of one of those Chicago movies. He was a little man himself, beautifully dressed, wearing gloves, sallow-faced with flat, dark eyes, and he stared at her father across the open grave.

After the funeral — and Chone told her this calmly — he and her father, who were at the corner of St. Catherine and Mountain, had started to walk up the hill to the Ritz. It was about noontime. A car stopped beside them, three men got out, one of them slugged her father on the head, the other two started clubbing Chone. Her father, a big, opulent man, stood stunned, and the guy stepped back, waiting for him to fall into his arms so he could drag him into the car; and he did spin slowly on his heel, then he shook his head to clear it, and he grabbed his assailant in a bear hug and threw him over the hood of the car. Chone said he himself had been slashed across the face . . . "See, here," he said, indicating a long cut on his cheek which was healing. The two guys who were on him, he said, left him, grabbed the third one, and got into their car and fled. Chone said he took her father to the hospital because he was afraid of a concussion. At the hospital they X-rayed him. He was all right. Just a bump as big as a melon on his head.

While he was in the hospital, Whitey Unger, a poor, guilt-ridden, tormented man, came to see him.

"You'll never testify," he said angrily. "Run if you want to, Mr. Bixby. Look, you have a daughter and they know about her. So you won't be testifying." Her father got a priority on a plane for England.

Telling her these things sitting in the lounge at the Algonquin, Jethroe Chone had a very hard glint in his eyes.

"Make it as fast as you can, Miss Gina," he said. "I'm to get you out of the country — to your father in England. That's the word and it's up to me."

"Oh, it is, is it?" she said. Well, he wasn't telling her what to do and when to do it. Who did he think he was to be taking charge of her? Supposing she didn't want to go to England? And besides, she didn't feel she was in any danger. He just smiled and was silent. He waited, and she felt herself struggling with him and getting outraged. She began to talk down her nose to him. His face got red, he just put up with it. As far as he was concerned, she had no choice. Really, she could have slapped him.

"I'm going out now," she said. "I'll think it over. I'll call you at the Waldorf."

"Okay. Just be ready, Miss Gina," he said, and she walked out on him.

On the morning of the third day she had got up late and was walking east on 44th to a little lunch counter named Louie's to have some toast and coffee. She had a luncheon appointment. Before she could enter the lunch counter, a car which must have been following her stopped, and two men, getting out, apparently to go into Louie's, wheeled around, grabbed her, and hustled her toward their car. She screamed. A little old man, a dwarf with a very big round head, happened to be passing, and he swung his cane and tripped her and the two men. They all rolled on the sidewalk. Customers running out of the restaurant grabbed at her. There was a lot of yelling and cursing, and the two men got away. She gave the little dwarf, who was known to everyone in the neighborhood, a ten-dollar bill and a kiss on his bald head, and went back to the hotel and stayed in the room.

Early in the afternoon, Jethroe Chone came around, as she knew he would, and she admitted she was scared. He got a car. Late that afternoon they headed for the Cape where her father had a place near Wellfleet. On the drive to Boston they hardly talked to each other, yet she felt safe with him. They stayed overnight at a Boston hotel. He seemed to like what he was doing. She felt his tremendous confidence. He was so calm and gentle with her, she lost her fear. They drove on to Wellfleet. She had always liked the dunes and the pines and the sea. An elderly painter, a Yale man she was fond of, lived nearby, and she wanted to talk to him, and went by herself through the pines; when she was near a cemetery she saw Jethroe Chone coming through the pines after her, looking big, lonely, and threatening.

"For God's sake, leave me alone a minute. Beat it, Jethroe. Give me time to sort things out." She talked to him as if he were her father's boy. That's all he was, anyway. It was all he had ever been. But she went back to the house with him.

Early that evening they saw a car coming up the drive. Two men got out and approached the house. Jethroe Chone made a motion to her to be silent. In the hall, in the brass stand, was one

94

of those heavy Irish blackthorn sticks with a big knob on the end, and when the men came to the door, even before they could knock, Jethroe Chone swung the door open and leaped out swinging the heavy black cane. They howled in pain, dragging themselves back to their car, and then they were gone, and she gave up arguing about getting to England and her father.

"Well, now you know who 'they' are," she said, looking directly at Ira Groome.

"I see," he said. He was trying to take it all in. "Look," he said abruptly, "Chone must be mad. Rosso and the U-boat? Come on," and he looked up at the bridge. What would the Captain say to this?

"You just don't understand the temperament," she said, shrugging. "Maybe Jethroe picked up his frame of mind from my father. The gamblers, they get profound hunches about things, you know. Each day they have to find something that'll tell them how they stand with the world. No, not just the world. Something outside themselves . . . something out there. Little things tell them, and big things, too. Rosso tried to stop him or get hold of me. Right? And the U-boat sinks us. Right? So the U-boat is on Rosso's side, see? The war is fixed, too."

"Chone, eh?" he said. "So that's Chone."

"That's Chone, Ira."

"I suppose your father's lucky to have such a man."

"Don't worry, we have him. Body and soul." Her tone was so grim, he looked startled. The sun now was full on her face. Her eyes had always been narrowed, or turned away, and now he saw how dark they were, brown or black with flecks of green, the shade of a dark, threatening forest he had seen in Central America. Confused, he said, "I don't get it," and she saw he was confused, and with her slow smile she tried to mask her feeling.

"Get what?" she said.

"Well, I don't know," he said, his eyes on the deck, and then suddenly on her bare feet. The long toes, the instep, the foot so slender and white, the toes like fingers, then she moved her left foot. The bare foot! Then he became aware that in spite of being so sea-washed, so clean, a woman's scent, very faint and very sweet, came from her, and it struck him that she knew of and liked the dark roots of her blonde hair that showed at the part; she wanted that dark line to be there.

95

"Well — " he began hesitantly. Then he said, "My God . . . well, I have to go. In a few minutes it's my watch." He could see the Captain, the glasses to his eyes, showing concern as he talked to the mahogany-faced navigator. Something was bothering the Captain. Yet as he went to the bridge all he could think about was that Chone didn't give a damn about this war.

"How's that straggler, sir?" he said to the Captain.

"Look at that," said the Captain. The straggler had just belched up a plume of smoke. "Why the hell all that smoke?" the Captain said irritably. But there was just that one black plume trailing across the sky.

"Oh, that looks better," the Captain said, putting down the glasses. Now he could go to his cabin. Maybe he would have the steward bring him a pot of tea. Maybe he would offer Jethroe Chone a drink of rum.

"How do you find Mr. Chone, sir?" Ira Groome asked.

"No doubt about it, the man has been around," the Captain said. "Well, that's the investor's world for you. Sooner or later, they all have to turn to the bankers. Chone seems to have met all those theatrical people we read about. Very interesting. Had some good stories about Ingrid Bergman. Always liked her pictures myself. How about you? Do you like those Swedes?"

"I wish I had seen more of Greta Garbo, sir."

"A bit flat-chested, I always thought. Must ask Chone if he ever met her."

"I still would like to see more of her," he called to the Captain, who was leaving the bridge. Then he looked out over the water. Gina and Chone kept coming into his thoughts, and he was bent on putting them out of his mind. But just before he managed to do so, he thought of the French fighter, Riopelle, and how the boy had looked at his broken hands, and then it struck him that it was strange that the people in Gina's story had more reality for him than the enemy who was bent on destroying him and his comrades and all the ships. He hadn't met any of them face to face, but he hadn't met Riopelle either. He picked up the glasses. He went on watching the straggler that had belched up a plume of smoke. The ship was still falling back.

"There's something really the matter there," he said to the navigator. "I'm surprised we don't get a signal." But while the navigator was watching the faltering ship the signal to investi-

96

gate came from the destroyer. They turned back. Soon they were abreast of the tanker, and he hailed the tanker's master, who was on the bridge.

"Engine trouble," the master yelled. "The engineer has a fever, and we had a hell of a time getting him away from the engines. Everything should be all right now."

The sun, now an orange ball, rolled into the gray water rising slowly around it. The horizon crept in, the soft rolling seaswell became a polished slate, with all the gray ships keeping their smoke down and becoming one with the graying water. He watched the man in the asdic hut listening intently, for the sea was a living thing, not silent at all; all that stuff about the silent sea was nonsense, he thought. Anyone who listened to the asdic instruments knew how the sea had its flow of noisy traffic, its wild, screeching sea sound; a submerged habitation with its own flashing lights.

But during the middle watch he saw the rockets go up far astern and streak like a spray of comets across the sky. The U-boat had got the tanker. A flash of fire shot up on the horizon, the flash against the night sky flowering as the petals of a tiger lily open up in dark, soft, velvety streaks against the orange petals of fire; then it seemed to go rolling up in a gigantic spray.

"There she goes," the Captain said bitterly. "There goes the oil." A kind of quiet fury was in the Captain. "We'll head back and do a sweep and see if we can pick up an echo from the U-boat," he said. But he couldn't take his eyes off the tanker. "From now on we'll have company," he said.

They did not head back towards the wide glow on the water where the tanker still burned, where men were struggling and dying in the oily water while the glow got smaller and smaller. They were not going to turn back to pick up survivors; another ship had got such a signal. The operator in the asdic hut was trying to get a contact from the U-boat while the Captain looked into the hut, but they couldn't get an echo. Far back, the tanker, still burning, sank slowly, the glow suddenly wiped away. And then there was nothing back there but the smooth streak of moonlit water.

TWELVE ~~~~~~~~~~~~~~~~~~~~~~~~

Then he was in the wardroom sitting in the Captain's place at the head of the little table. Woodruff, who had been stretched out on the settee, sat up when the steward brought in the pork chops and baked brown potatoes from the nearby galley.

"I'm so hungry that even those pork chops look good," Woodruff said. "Ah, this wonderful sea air does make any kind of cooking seem good."

Woodruff, a brave officer, was a charming scamp with a gift for making his malice sound attractive. Having had the money to move around the world, he liked talking about other countries and about the incredible perversions he had witnessed in Port

Said, and the sexual preferences of Malay girls. In France he had met André Gide. Woodruff, too, believed in the cult of experience. Leo Cawthra and Woodruff used to sit with Ira Groome and argue about Jean Cocteau and Gide, and wonder why Cocteau got blamed for doing the scandalous things that Gide did, while Gide himself remained a venerated figure.

"Have you talked to the girl yet, Woodruff?" he asked him.

"Of course, I have. I'm democratic. I talk to everyone. Eastern seaboard schools. A slightly déclassé debutante type."

"Oh, come on."

"She bleaches her hair."

"But how do you like her?"

"Of course, I like her. When that girl smiles it's easy time for everyone."

"Easy time?"

"A man feels at ease with himself and the world. It's what it's all about, isn't it, Ira?"

"I suppose it is." And then Jethroe Chone came in.

"Gentlemen," Chone said gravely, and he sat down with them. "Tell me something, gentlemen," he said.

"Go ahead, Mr. Chone," Ira said, believing Chone was going to express some concern about the U-boat on the horizon.

"You call the Captain 'the old man'. Why 'the old man'?"

"A naval custom. That's all."

"If it were an Irish ship I suppose we'd call the Captain 'himself'," Woodruff said.

"Himself. I see. Why not call him just 'the man'?"

"The man. Hmm," Ira said. "Sounds like . . . " and suddenly Chone's slow, careful speech began to annoy him; he wanted to hear him slip into tough phrases coming out of the corner of his mouth; he wanted to say something that would make Chone wonder if he had really taken him in. Yet in fairness to Gina he had to be cautious.

"It depends on the business you're in, I suppose, Mr. Chone," he said. "Would you feel more at home if we called the Captain 'the man'?"

"Yes, sir," Chone said calmly.

"Mr. Chone is in the investment banking business, Woodruff. Do you call Mr. Bixby 'the man', Mr. Chone?"

"Someone is always 'the man'."

"Oh? What bank, Mr. Chone?" Woodruff asked.

"Bixby and Partners," Chone said calmly.

"Wall Street?"

"Sure. London and Paris, too," Chone said.

"There you are, Woodruff. Now, if you have a little money —"

"Everyone likes to make a little money," Chone said. But his watchful gaze did not shift away from him to Woodruff. It was as if he was challenging him while lying so brazenly. Picking up a piece of bread, Chone began to butter it.

"This sea air makes me very hungry," he said.

"I know something about the English money market," Woodruff said. "I had an uncle with Lloyds . . . "

"Name of Woodruff?" Chone asked.

"No. Morrow. Algernon T. Morrow."

"We've had a connection with Lloyds," Chone said. "But this time we aren't seeing the bankers."

"No?"

"Mr. Bixby . . . "

"The girl's father, Woodruff."

"Yeah, Miss Bixby's father," Chone said, putting a well-buttered piece of bread in his mouth. "You see, there is to be a new British purchasing agent in Washington."

"Ah, I see."

"Mr. Bixby is being consulted," he said, a flicker of amusement in his hard, watchful eyes. He was kidding them, having suspected, or perhaps having known, that Gina had revealed his relationship with Mr. Bixby and his mission. His effrontery was astonishing. The Captain could be told about him and he knew it. In his massive calmness and in the slow movement of his jaw chomping on a crust of bread, Chone was telling him that he didn't care what he thought of him or what he did about it.

THIRTEEN

In the morning when the air was heavy and wet with a fog coming up, they caught a glimpse of the U-boat. It was just a speck on the horizon seen through the glasses about five miles back, acting as a lure to draw the escort vessels away from the convoy, so other U-boats could sneak in among the ships. All day it was there on the horizon, and as he padded along the deck, his uninflated Mae West flapping against his blue sweater, he kept looking alertly at the hands doing their work. He saw leading seaman Henderson come on deck and turn warily to look back at the U-boat. They were all doing it now. And yet Jethroe Chone came parading along the deck with Gina with all the aplomb he would have had promenading down Fifth Avenue. What made me so sure she needed my concern, Ira Groome wondered.

"You two should be wearing your lifebelts, you know," he called out abruptly on his way to the bridge. "Put them on."

"Oh, I'm sorry, Lieutenant," she called.

"You don't have to keep them inflated. Just wear them."

"We'll remember, Lieutenant," Chone said. "Thank you. Just an oversight," and he made a courteous little bow.

The man was baffling. Even the Captain had said Chone was either recklessly brave, or recklessly indifferent; he couldn't be just sublimely unaware, and yet there was something rather magnificent about him. "In a way it's nice having Mr. Chone around," the Captain had said. "Don't you think so?"

As he came on the bridge he heard the Captain saying to the man in the asdic hut, "How's the contact?"

"I think I've still got it, sir."

"See what you can hear, No. 1."

The scratching little hollow ping was like the beating of a heart, only not muffled like a heart; it came throbbing in the vastness of cathedral space.

"It's there, sir," he called, and the Captain joined him. No one on the bridge moved until the Captain, suddenly stepping out of the asdic hut, ordered depth charges to be prepared, then turned to him.

"Sound action stations," he said quietly. But even as the rattle clanged he knew by the way the Captain pulled a handkerchief out of his pocket and wiped his mouth that he didn't quite believe they had actually contacted the submarine. There was an awful pounding and din along the deck and on the ladders, and shouted orders from Horler the bosun, mixed with the short, encouraging yelping of the hands streaming on deck as they inflated their lifebelts and jumped to their battle stations, while leading seaman Henderson, at the big gun, yelped and cursed, working himself into a frenzy. Closed at the action stations, the men waited, while the operator in the asdic hut listened. They all seemed to be following the pinging with the beating of their own hearts. At least ten minutes passed before the Captain came out of the asdic hut.

"Maybe it was a whale," he said. And the operator said, "I'd have sworn it wasn't, sir."

"You still think it was a U-boat? Well, you've got a great ear," but he gave the order, "Pipe secure," and then they all shared a sudden sense of ease. He liked moving around the ship at such times. All the hands became gay, laughing, brawling, kidding comrades. Some took it easy on deck. Others went down to their quarters to get some sleep. The green hands were the most excited; their voices a little louder, they wanted to relax a little more exuberantly. As he was going aft, stopping from time to time to look over the side at the darkening water, he saw Gina and Chone laughing, as everyone was laughing, and they were talking to Mason. He beckoned to Mason.

"How does Miss Bixby take this action station stuff?"

"It scares the wits out of her," Mason said.

"She should be one of the hands by now."

"Well, she's not. But that guy's crazy."

"How so?"

"I'd swear he enjoys it."

"I think he does. Yes, he does — "

"And I think the men like to do little things for Miss Bixby."

"Not much they can do, Mason."

"You saw that nice-looking white shirt she wears?"

"A man's shirt?"

"Right. The steward got it for her."

"He did? I wonder whose it was. Well, what about the thing she probably misses most?"

"What's that, sir?"

"A lipstick."

"I think I can get her a lipstick from Henderson."

"If he can't get anything else from a girl he can at least get her lipstick. Trophies. I'll see."

In the mid-afternoon of the next day, when he was thinking of having a cup of coffee, he noticed that a group of stokers had come up from the engine room. Usually the stokers kept to themselves; they would come rushing up from the engine room at nightfall, get washed up, then they would eat, go back to their quarters and fall asleep. Now they went slowly to the rail where they stood looking out over the water. They were always the first ones to feel impending trouble. While he was watching them, Chone came along the deck with his annoying troubled air.

"Look, stokers, Mr. Chone. Watch them, Mr. Chone."

"Why them, sir?"

"They usually don't act like that. Maybe they feel things coming, Mr. Chone."

"Yeah, I notice things myself," Chone said. "Interesting. Very interesting. Everybody goes around like a cat now. Everything quiet and peaceful and everybody sort of creeping around," and then he grinned. "Soon I'll start creeping around myself. How many days from shore, sir?"

"Well, we keep altering course."

"Three? Four?"

"Maybe more."

"Right now, sir — if you'll excuse this — the steward is bringing some tea and biscuits to Miss Bixby in the sick bay. She's a little tense. And everybody around here is tense, and I thought — if you are relaxing now, it would give her a big lift — make everything seem normal — if you could have a cup of tea with her — with us?"

His slow, careful style seemed to give dignity to his concern for Gina. The strange blue eyes meeting his and holding them seemed to be saying dignified things. His red beard had grown.

"Why yes, I'd like to have a cup of tea," he said, and he accompanied Chone to the sick bay. She was there. He was sure she looked relieved.

"Thanks for the lipstick, Lieutenant," she said. "See, I've got it on." And then with a nervous little laugh she said, too brightly, "The steward says he's bringing in a big pot of tea. But how do we all sit down?"

"On the deck," he said. "Like this," and he squatted on the matting over the steel deck. "Mr. Chone and I like this. You on the bunk. That's right. There you are," and he was only a few feet away from her dangling bare foot. It was hanging there, touched by sunlight.

"Yeah, this is great," Chone said, making himself comfortable with a very satisfied grin. The steward brought in the tray holding the tea, the hot water, the cups, and some biscuits, and placed it on the stationary little table beside the bunk. Very sedately she poured the tea.

"The steward makes a pretty good cup of tea, don't you think?" he asked. "Just a little sugar, please, Miss Bixby."

"You really do like tea, sir?" Chone asked.

"We drank it at home, when I was a boy," he said. "Just a little more hot water, please." Pouring the water, she had the gracious lady-like tea-party air, though they were far out on the Atlantic.

"It fascinates me that a man like you can be so easily a part of this naval routine," she said. "How do you manage to fit in so well?"

"Just do the best I can."

"Come on, Lieutenant."

"No, it was the one memorable bit of advice, my father, a doctor, passed on to me."

"To do the best you can," she repeated. "Well, when do you sit down and say, 'I can stop giving my best. Now I've made it'?"

"When you get to the right place, I suppose."

"And where is the right place — Yucatan," as if it didn't matter that Chone wouldn't know what they were talking about; he was ignorant; he was Red Chone, the pool hustler. Yet Chone nodded and grinned. Leaning back on the palms of his huge hands, he stretched out his legs, crossing them at the ankles.

Was she back in that story he had told her about the Mayan girl, he wondered. What did she want him to tell her about those nights in that village? Or was she trying to see him, hear him talking to the girl? He began to tell about a long-forgotten well filled with skulls, sacrificial skulls, sacrifice piled on sacrifice. It had made him wonder about the terrible need of sacrifice. He did not notice that her silent wonder, and the intense interest in her eyes, had made him forget that they were in the middle of the North Atlantic. Nor did he hear the voices of seamen passing on the flats outside the sick bay. Nor did he notice that Chone, utterly relaxed as he was, would look at him then at her changing face. She looked as if she were far away and lonely. Wondering why, he paused, holding his breath.

"I'd like to go to the Yucatan," she said dreamily. "I'd like to have been there with you," and meditating, she nodded, then came leaning closer; the tips of the fingers of her right hand were rubbing delicately against her thumb. He seemed to feel the fingers touch his own skin. Her dreaming eyes had dropped, they were on her bare foot, and as he looked at her naked feet and ankles, the bareness of her feet made the rest of her that he had seen on the bunk in this room come vividly into his imagination. He had to find satisfaction for his hard desire, yet there could only be words now.

"There was a city called Tula," he said. "It was one of those magic cities, a place of light. All through history these links of light in the dark chain of history. Links of warm light." As she listened so raptly he felt he was bringing her brushing against him, and he was using just words, words that were not even sensual. He had never shared such a feeling with a woman.

"Tell me . . . tell me . . . yes, that's right, that's right. Ah, that's right," she said softly, her eyes on him as he talked; and then she hesitated, as if she were afraid of saying something she didn't want to say. "That city. That Toltec city. Tula," she said erratically. "I wouldn't mind being called Tula. Why wasn't I called Tula?" And he could feel her struggling against herself, or Chone, or her father, and then the sea and the jungle seemed to be in her eyes and he felt himself racing away with her.

"I'm still here," Chone said calmly.

"What? Oh, yeah."

"What's the matter with her own name — Gina?" Chone asked.

"That's right," he said awkwardly. What had been going on between him and Gina was so shamelessly apparent, Ira wanted to say something to put her at ease. But she was looking at Chone, then back at him, almost furtively, as if she had betrayed herself and was frightened.

"You'd like to go to Yucatan, wouldn't you, Jethroe?" she said, and put her hand on Chone's shoulder.

"I don't think so," Chone said. "I don't know anything about Yucatan," and he remained comfortably stretched out on the deck. Though he was patting Gina's hand, Chone's eyes still were full of amused, indulgent approval.

"That's all right, Mr. Chone," he said. Confused, he stood up.

"Anyway, it's very interesting. Very interesting," Chone said. "Eh Gina?" as if he recognized her need of this kind of distraction or anything else that could take her mind off the straits they were in.

"You're an entertaining talker, sir," Chone said.

"Thanks," he said crisply. The voices from seamen passing the door came to them:

"It's a lot of crap."

106

"Well, fuck you then."

"Crap, I said, crap."

"And I say, fuck you."

And Gina was saying something to him with her eyes.

"I have to go, you know," he said. "This has been very nice. Thank you," and he left. He found Chone fantastic. "The crazy son of a bitch," he said to himself. "He's not even in this world. He's right out of some old western." It was amusing. Chone in a movie; a man who started out on a stagecoach on a journey with a lovely woman through wild Indian country. Outlaws had wrecked their coach, they had been picked up by another one, now again they were in hostile country, and while the stage rolled along, he was grateful if one of the no-account stagecoach hands could keep Miss Bixby amused.

FOURTEEN 〰〰〰〰〰〰〰〰〰〰〰〰

The fog, drifting toward the ship in fleece-like little banks, rolled around him like smoke belching from a thousand chimneys and when it broke there were strips of dark polished ebony paths through the hidden world of shadowy mists. These beckoning, hard watery paths shone momentarily in a strange cold light and he saw her on one of those paths; he heard friendly voices come out of the fog.

"Hello, Miss Bixby," or "Hey, stop a minute, why don't you?" and he saw one shadowy figure, then another one, brush against her. And there was Boseley on the monkey bridge, the port lookout, apparently watching the water, yet letting his eyes follow one of those clear lanes through the fog on the deck till he saw Miss Bixby. She was alone now, sitting on a pile of rope near the depth-charge rail, an elbow on her knee, her chin in her hand as the ship swayed and dipped and the crests of the waves reached up around her in a restless, unfulfilled caressing motion, and when he appeared beside her, she said,

"Hello, Ira Groome. Tell me something. Where are we?"

"On the wing of a convoy."

"I can't see any ships."

"In this kind of fog, no."

"Aren't we ever going to land?"

"Oh, I think so."

"What port are we heading for?"

"It depends."

"Doesn't anyone know?"

"Oh, I think so."

"The men move around in the fog like ghosts."

"Take a look at them as soon as the fog lifts."

"I was thinking of you," she said. Off by herself she went to speak. Then hesitated. "Look, when we land, if we land . . . "

"I could get to London," he said.

"You mean it?"

"I think so. I can be with you in London."

"Ira — can I count on it? Really?"

"Yes, Gina. What are you afraid of?"

"Me? Nothing. Why?"

"Is it Chone — in London?"

"Ira — I'm not afraid of Chone. I just like to think you and I can be together in London."

"Mr. Chone doesn't intimidate me in the slightest, Gina."

"He's not trying to, Ira. Really he isn't," she said, sounding worried.

"Then it's dinner for us — the two of us, in London."

"If it's what you want, I'd love it Ira. I'm going to count on it," she said. "Yes," as if she had convinced herself that she had to be with him in London.

"I know you don't know much about me, Gina," he said, "and yet —"

"I know," she said after a moment, softly and simply. "How long does it take? Do we ever know? If I don't know this at once,

109

then I don't think I can ever really know. But if we do know in this world, then we should seize the time of knowing. I feel so safe, so right about myself when you're around."

"Won't Chone be around in London?"

"No, he won't."

"You said he was always there with your father."

"He'll be where my father wants him to be."

"In spite of all that magnificent assurance, eh? Did he always have it? Is that naturally the way he is?"

"No."

"No?"

"He's carried away now. Carried away. I mean . . . " In the fog he could hardly see her face, but the break in her voice, the hesitation, told him she was trying to hold back.

"The change in Jethroe Chone . . . well, it's a joke," she said harshly. "Maybe he never knew who he was, nor what he was, so he took it out with a lot of clowning. Sometimes, when I was around, he'd talk tough as if, well, deliberately reminding me of his hoodlum background. Next time I saw him he'd be talking slowly like a gentle professor. In fact some of my father's crowd used to call him 'the Professor'. He likes it. I guess he's always felt out of place."

"Out of place?"

"No. Well, not exactly. I mean, it got that he no longer knew his place."

"Look, Gina, what is it with you and Jethroe Chone?"

"I'll tell you later, Ira."

"Tell me now."

"Do you know that since I started out from New York . . . "

"With Chone?"

"Yes, and all along the way I haven't had a chance to talk about this with anyone."

"You were on the run."

"Just Jethroe and me, never near anyone. Then you. And this is strange, Ira, not talking about it with you has been making me feel terribly lonely. Ira — I can hardly see you. You're just a shadow there." Then the fog patch drifted by, they could see each other, and the way she stared at him moved him.

"Gina," he said. But she blurted out, "I'll tell you what it is with me and Jethroe Chone, and what's going on now, and why it's going on."

"Good," he said, and waited. Then he wondered if she still wanted to be half-hidden from him, for soon she was and she took control of herself, and though she was just a shadow, her face sometimes clearly there, and sometimes hidden, the voice was clear, the lovely voice making everything she said so clear to him.

"You have to know what Jethroe Chone is like," she said evenly. "I know I've told you something about his background. Well, there's more." Then she told him that Chone had come from somewhere in Brooklyn, where he had lived in poverty with his mother. He used to hang around Stillman's gym where the fighters train, doing odd jobs. He was a pool hustler, too. Maybe he had thought of being a fighter himself, being such a powerful, barrel-chested man with so much fierce energy. In Stillman's he had met her father, whom he supplied with gambling information. He did it regularly. And maybe there was something compelling about him. He had those wild, hard eyes and a lot of courage, and an instinct that drove him toward a man like her father, whom he respected enormously. Not only because her father was rich, but because he had the gambler's life, and at the same time was a cultivated man who commanded respect. Her father dressed beautifully. He went to the theater, he read books. In fairness to Chone, he would have given his life for her father. Once or twice he nearly did.

As for her, only when she was at college did she get to know Jethroe. Then, bit by bit, she could see him changing. His speech, for one thing. At first she thought he was clowning, trying to amuse her by mimicking her father, and she always laughed. He went on with it, he got better at it. She had to laugh, then one day she saw the hurt in his crazy, proud, lonely eyes and she stopped laughing.

One weekend when Chone drove her back to Smith, he borrowed books from her. He was reading. He said very little, but she knew he looked down his nose at a lot of stuff she read.

"They don't know anything," he said. "That guy D. H. Lawrence. Polly Adler could look after him."

"I don't know why I stopped laughing. I should have kept on laughing," she said and brooded, and he waited, saying nothing. He felt that she was trying to see his face. She couldn't, so she went on.

111

She had noticed that people now were afraid to cross Chone. The careful speech, the big, powerful manicured hands, the clothes like her father's, and the growing pride in his bearing only added to the threat you felt in him, which was very valuable in his job as her father's bodyguard. He knew so well he belonged to her father, it was almost frightening. And he was too protective of her. If she had a college man with her when they were in a place like Lindy's with her father, and her college friend got affectionate, Jethroe Chone tried to scare him off. She had to tell him to mind his own business.

That night at the Cape, she said, when they got into the car, they had no plan. For an hour, sitting beside her in the car, Jethroe Chone brooded and planned. Outside Boston, he called a New York chef, a gambling man who knew her father. This chef had a stone house in Bucks County, in Pennsylvania, near the Delaware, just across the river from Frenchtown. It was a five-hundred-mile trip, and it took thirteen hours' driving. All night they drove. Sometimes he stopped to make phone calls. In the middle of the night they crossed the Delaware on one of those covered bridges, and followed the river road, and turned up a red dirt road. She could remember the redness of the dirt in the headlights and the way the bushes had their leaves turned back. They came to an old stone house near a magnificent huge stone barn. When they were getting out of the car, he told her that the chef had an architect looking at the barn who had plans to turn it into the showplace of the countryside. The stone house had small rooms fixed up nicely. She took one of the rooms and fell sound asleep. In the morning he made her her breakfast, and told her they were only about seventy-five miles from New York, and he had to go into town. She would be safe here, and he would return early in the evening. All that day she felt secure enough to bathe in the little stream and go into the woods, where she saw a deer. Only when it got dark was she nervous. By keeping Jethroe Chone in her mind all the time, she overcame the nervousness. By ten he had returned. In two days they would sail from Boston, he said. He had always called her Miss Gina. Now he was calling her just Gina.

"All these little things are important," she said. "I have to tell them if you're to see the thing," and now she began to talk more rapidly. Chone had brought some food and two bottles of

112

Beaujolais, she said, and it was almost like a little, lazy family dinner. He talked about the luck he had had with some investments her father had made for him; he had a bank account in Zurich, and about baseball.

"I remember I asked him if he didn't intend to get married," she said, "and if there was a special girl." "None of those broads who hang around are special," he said. "You learn this when you're alone with them saying nothing and doing nothing. That is the way to learn."

When it got dark the house was damp and chilly, even though it was warm enough outside, and he got some firewood and two big logs. Soon they had a fire going in the big hearth, and they drank a little wine, and from time to time she got up and poked at the fire, and when you're comfortable and a little drowsy you get into the habit of simply staring at the flame, and you don't need to talk to the one who is there with you. She had got up once to poke at the ashes and move the log, and when the flame shot up the light flicked on his face, that face so vivid in its dreaming concentration. It was as if in their silence, sitting there, he felt they had said a hundred things that he was mulling over. And they didn't break the silence, and she got very drowsy, then she said,

"Well, I'm going to bed, Jethroe." Off by himself, he didn't answer. She remembered that when she looked back he was still staring at the last of the flames from the log.

In bed she watched the moonlight on the deep casement window, and heard some night birds, then the rustle of some small animal hurrying over the roof. No sound came from downstairs, where Jethroe Chone sat by the fire, sat and dreamed while the log glowed, then turned into ashes. She fell asleep, then woke up suddenly; her head was turned so she could see the window; she thought a shadow had passed across the window, and didn't know how this could happen unless a bird kept swooping by. Then she was aware of another presence, a kind of chill on her neck, a tightening in her stomach, and she thought Rosso's men had followed, and yelled "Jethroe!", and sat up.

Chone was there at the side of the bed, the window light on him, and he was naked, silent and naked.

"My God," she said, then froze in wonder and disbelief, for

113

he was taking her head in his hands, turning her head so the moonlight would be on it; this night light was on his face too. Then she got hold of herself.

"What the hell is this? Are you out of your mind? Get out of here," she said curtly. When he didn't answer, she tried to sound bored and irritated. "Don't be so damned silly. Really, what a presumptuous fool you are." He neither moved nor answered.

"Are you really such a disgusting lout? Oh, you idiot."

And she tried to swing out of the bed. In those hills a wild scream couldn't have helped her. Grabbing her by the wrists, he slowly pinned her down. His breathing wasn't hoarse or desperate, but very even, very sure in its rhythm. It was this that suddenly terrified her. He held her down with one hand, and, using the other, tore the nightdress off her. She kept jabbing at his eyes and tearing at his neck and biting him. He was too strong, he was on her. Then, in the crazy room shadows coming from the swaying branches of trees in the window light, she shouted,

"You pig. Gutter rat. Just wait. God help you." Then she let herself go flat. Cold and dead. She thought he had too much pride to possess a dead woman. He took his time. The thing, the awful thing was that gradually she felt, well, overwhelmed.

When he finished with her she had to wait to come back to herself; the hatred of herself on the bed in this condition, it tore at her heart. A part of her had been killed, and no one could understand this, this killing of a part of her. When she became herself she started to tremble with a rage that became an agonizing pain. A man can't understand this. The brutal taking of something that was even more than herself.

And yet he was standing beside her. Without saying a word, he left her. Then she cried and did not hate herself for crying. It helped harden the rage in her, it helped her to understand that, for the time being, there was nothing to do but cry quietly. She saw how trapped she was. If she ran from him now and got back to the city, she couldn't go to the police. Aside from the demeaning approach they would take to her, which would be unbearable, any kind of publicity would be noticed by Rosso's men and they would try again to grab her. If the police came into it, Chone would not be around. Then it seemed likely to her that in the morning Jethroe would come to his senses, realize how he

114

had betrayed her father's trust, get scared, and run. Jethroe knew how ruthless her father could be. He might not even be there in the morning. Or he might even come crawling to her begging forgiveness, or even try to kill himself — since his loyalty to her father was ground into his bones. In the morning she might find that he had fled, never to be seen again.

She remembered that she slept fitfully, and as soon as she woke up she heard him downstairs, in the kitchen. The sudden intensity of her rage unnerved her. From her bag she got a long nail file and put it in her pocket.

When she went downstairs she found he had their breakfast on the table. He was making coffee.

"Good morning, Gina," he said quietly. "Sit down," and then he turned, "Look, do you think that post office store down by the river road would have the newspaper. Should I run down and see?" He was calm, almost dignified, not even a furtive glance at her.

Finally she said,

"What are you going to do?"

"What do you mean?" he asked.

"Where are you going?"

In genuine surprise, he said, "Why, to Boston. Aren't we sailing?" She couldn't believe it. No remorse in him, and he proposed to go with her to her father. That was his job. Nothing was going to interfere. His faithful obedience, his calmness about it, stunned her. If he had grabbed her, threatening her, and insisted on heading for South America or someplace, she would have understood it. His loyalty to his boss made his brutal assault on her seem more menial. Even though he was playing into her hands, she half-despised his sense of servitude that would take him on to the end. She knew she would have to nurse him along. So she became as casual as he was. Not a word was said about last night, though she knew the ugly thing was in his mind, for he was getting pleasure out of being gentle with her, as if he was now entitled to express this gentleness. And sometimes she couldn't believe he was actually coming along with her. Not till they actually sailed.

The ship rolled a little, a siren wail came from the engine-room pump, and he said, "What does Chone think will happen?"

115

"I don't think he cares," she said.

"What will happen?"

"Well, he'll be told to go back home."

"Will he go?"

"Oh, he'll do what he's told to do."

"And then?"

"You don't know my father. Jethroe Chone will be killed." She did not sound like a college girl. "For a thousand dollars you can get anybody killed, a phone call will do it," she said quietly. For a moment, as thick wads of fog shifted, she was in one of those clear lanes, and he caught a glimpse of the grim, hard set of her jaw. But as the clear lane was filled again with that white stuff rolling around them she became hardly more than a shadow.

"There's just one thing," he began, but she had stood up. She had moved away from him as if she knew that he wanted to say, "If you know what will happen and even look forward to it with such satisfaction, what are you afraid of now?" Instead, following her, he called softly, "Gina, Gina," but when he was beside her at the rail, she didn't turn. "It's all right," he said. He understood that in telling him the story she had been trying to bring Chone out of some tormenting secret place in her heart, to get him out where he could be looked at, so she could feel he would go out of her life.

Here in the fog, at the rail, he could safely take her arm, the arm that was close to him, and he held it against him. But as soon as he drew her close like this he felt her tremble with emotion. At other times she had been self-possessed. Any time she had appeared on deck she had been smiling and ready with her gallant air. "You'll be in London with me, won't you, Ira?" She said urgently. It was as if she had said, "You'll be with me after Chone is gone, won't you?" And her emotion made him feel that for her, Chone's death had already happened. She made him feel it with such certainty that he could see himself a month later in some hotel reading an item in the newspaper about a man named Jethroe Chone found badly beaten in some alley, then shot to death, and he was moved now as he would be then.

"I guess he had it coming to him," he said.

"Don't waste your time feeling sorry for him," she said grimly. But she clutched at his arm; her fingers dug into him.

"And we'll be in London, and we'll be together, won't we? Won't we, Ira Groome? You're different. I could be at ease with you, Ira." And it was as if she was trying very hard to see herself with him ashore and couldn't — no matter how hard she tried.

"Oh, Ira, Why not? Why not?" and again her fingers tightened on his arm. And he felt that in trying to make it real and certain and thus end some struggle within herself, she would have hurled herself into his arms there at the rail. Then, as fog thick as a snow bank came around them again, she slid away ten feet along the rail as if waiting to see if he had to follow her.

"Just a minute," he said, and she let him come brushing against her. "I'm here with you, Gina," he said. "I'm never far away. Don't feel lonely. I know how lonely you are here on this ship with the things that have happened. It's the lonely and terrible time in your life. This is no place for me to say things to you. We'll really be together in London. . . . Really, Gina, really." Then, over her shoulder, he saw a figure coming along the deck, and as if by instinct she turned. At first it was just a heavy dark blob in the fog, then the figure loomed up, heavy-shouldered. It was Chone.

"Don't say anything to him," she whispered quickly.

"He should keep out of the sick bay."

"I can handle him," she said.

FIFTEEN

And yet at nightfall, leaving the bridge to catch a few hours'
sleep, he heard her laughter coming from the port side, the laugh
coming easily. Then he heard Chone laugh too. He couldn't believe his ears. What kind of a woman was she, he wondered,
standing there laughing with the man who had degraded her?
Did she like it? And Chone seemed to be saying to him, "Hey,
does she look like she was raped?" Now he could hear them
talking to two of the hands. Chone was saying, "When we land,
I can't ask you all to dinner, but why not one big party? A
champagne party?" And the hand's voice, "Can I skip the champagne, Mr. Chone, and have a little rum or rye?" and they all

118

laughed. Now he could see them going along the deck, Chone holding her arm, and suddenly Chone's big hand on her offered an insight that moved him deeply. Chone had her under some kind of spell. "How the hell does he do it? Where does he get this power?" he thought; and, turning away, he glanced up at the lookouts silhouetted there like lonely stone-carved figures. And he saw Boseley's head bob; Boseley who had told some of the hands that the sound from the engine-room pump, when he was up there in the monkey bridge, always reminded him of the moaning of the wind in the telegraph wires at home in the Ottawa Valley, and he shouted irritably,

"Boseley!"

"Yes, sir."

"Watch yourself. Close your eyes again and you'll be thrown into detention."

"Yes, sir."

At the foot of the bridge ladder the navigator said,

"You're wasting your time, No. 1. You won't make a sailor out of the guy."

"If I can't, it means the little slob has licked me. He should never have left his taxicab."

"I heard him say he's not going back to it. He's going to be a bookie."

"Not for long. It'll be jail, or his taxi," he said.

Free now to relax and unwind before sleeping, he took his time. Mocking curses and jokes were coming from seamen sprawled out on mats under the gun turret, and he listened. In his broad Yorkshire accent, the English merchant seaman was telling the hands about women. He was good. The women of many countries had passed through his hands, he said, and though the seamen jeered and mocked him, they wanted him to go on, they wanted to believe that he could tell them the difference between French girls and Italian girls, and was it true that he really had met Margot, the fabulous whore from Calcutta?

"Ah, but the Portuguese girls," he said. "Pray to God you get to Portugal." And he told about a family in Lisbon who had a fifteen-year-old daughter and what had happened when he stayed with this family.

"Limey, you're a goddamned liar." Was that the signalman's voice? The stoker Briggs? No. Stokers kept to themselves.

119

"A line of crap as high as a telephone pole." The burst of laughter faded as the Yorkshireman protested.

"As God is my witness. The Portuguese women are like this."

"Let him go on," someone said. All the seamen on the mats really wanted him to go on giving them lovely dreams of new shores on the other side. It happened in Lisbon, he went on. There the mothers are harsh and strict with their daughters. The girls go in for black stockings. He had been staying in the home of this Portuguese sailor, who had this fifteen-year-old sister, a dear little doll. The family was poor, and a rich elderly grocer was after the little sister. But the old guy had told the mother that sweet little virgins frightened him. If the little girl was experienced, he could marry her. So the mother, God bless her — she called him "the dear Englishman" — was aware that he was a man who had known women in all the ports of the world; he could teach a little girl how to open up like a flower. As God was his witness, the mother asked him to take the girl to bed, and he did, again and again, till she had enough experience to delight the rich old grocer. The cunning old mother was happy because she knew her dear good Englishman would be sailing away, far away from the grocer and the girl. That was it.

Again there was laughter and jeering, then a silence. With night coming on and the sea quiet after a day that had been all monotony, a man dreamed of new, fantastic things awaiting him when he got ashore.

The fog had lifted. It was going to be a clear night with a new moon; the ship would be sailing against the moon. He wanted to see Chone. And then when he was on the lower deck he wondered why he wanted Chone to see him. Not talk to him. Just see him. Let Chone wonder how much he knew about him.

Now he could hear the hands in the mess deck, all irritable now. The morning after the ship had slipped at Halifax the hands had all been singing. Now, no singing and little horseplay. It was all up and down and eating and sleeping. A gramophone record had been playing, the needle grinding on and scratching the record. No one bothered to take it off.

"Take the damned thing off. I'm trying to write a letter," someone shouted: then the strumming of a guitar, the strumming listless, lazy.

"Hey, get a drum, why don't you?" Then he heard the bosun, Horler's voice, cursing, calling them a poor yelping bunch
of bastards, and then Horler came to the door of the mess deck.

"See Mr. Chone around, Horler?" he asked casually.

"Not for a while," Horler said. "You know, he's a great guy,
No. 1. Comes into the mess deck and talks to the guys about
baseball and the fights, and he's seen them all. The guy talks our
language, too. Not like a big business man at all."

"Yeah, a remarkable man, Horler," he said. "No doubt
about it." And then, as if drawn to the neighborhood of the sick
bay, approaching the flats he heard voices:

"You really think he's laying her in there?"

"Well, what in hell do you think he's doing?"

"I don't think he's laying her."

"You wanna bet?"

"I'll take a bet."

"What do you bet?"

"How do you prove this? What do we do? Ask her? " and
then they saw him, and Henderson, clearing his throat loudly,
went on.

"As I was saying, Bo, this war can't last forever, and I have
to remember I'm a radio announcer and should keep watching
my throat. A gargle, an announcer's secret, an aspirin gargle."

"Oh, come on, Henderson," he said, passing them, "that's
no radio announcer's secret. My grandmother used to use an aspirin gargle," and he went on to his own little cabin, leaving
them chuckling. Pulling off his sea boots, he stretched out in the
bunk, and while waiting for sleep to come he felt the need to understand his relationship with Gina and Chone, and his deepen-
ing concern for her. While the ship swayed and rolled he told
himself that his life ashore, and even here on the ship until his
hospitalization, had been ordinary and predictable. Now with
Gina and Chone he seemed to be on the edge of a world utterly
unlike the disciplined naval world; another world of violent personal passions.

Now he thought he saw something; no matter how Gina
acted when Chone was around, she wanted desperately to get
away from him. She had shown it. She had revealed it in those
intensely intimate moments when she had been with him at the
deck rail. He was sure that they had felt closer together in those

121

moments than some people feel in their whole lives. And how she had lit up at the thought of being with him in London; and this meant, of course, that she didn't quite believe Chone would be killed off. Maybe in Chone's presence and under his spell, she couldn't quite believe it, and that was why she was afraid and ready to run from Chone to him . . . if Chone would let her get away. His imagination was excited now, and in the dark he saw the curved instep of her bare foot and tried to recapture the faint scent on her skin. Gina! It was an odd name, Greek maybe? Eugena? Breasts like young oranges. And at each corner of her mouth just above the lip, tiny beauty marks, two very small black moles. And the other one, a tiny one, very low on her neck. And that twisting black tuft of pubic hair . . . that Chone had parted.

Jesus Christ, he whispered. Red Chone, the pool hustler, believing he now had some terrible hold on her. It was outrageous. And she was a fool, she was disgracing herself, letting a man like Chone make her feel compelled, not just to be submissive in his presence, but to laugh and be at ease. She did laugh. She did joke with him, and Chone — the man actually took it as his due. A hired thug, a man just a jump out of the hoodlum world. Yet Chone ought to be terrified. He ought to be dreading the end of the journey because she had all the advantages . . . unless Chone had recognized some fatal flaw in her. What was it?

And asking this, he became more fascinated as he tried to see her in the round, see her in her own life at college, where she would be prettier than most of them, and able to afford trips abroad and weekends in New York. The poetry! The clue might be in that poetry her school editors didn't like. Yes, the poetry, and quickening, he tried to see her on a weekend in her house at college at work on an essay on, say, T. S. Eliot and Gerard Manley Hopkins, and letting their images get into her mind and heart; ladies and white leopards and linden trees and ploughed-down silion shining. Literature; images that only made her restless, that only made her reach out recklessly for other kinds of rhythms and other kinds of raw and brutal and comic contrasts, and off she would go to New York for a night in her father's world. Another, rougher language. Grotesque heroes; on the fringe, the hoods, the promoters, the gamblers, and Jethroe Chone! Chone bent on making himself another man. On the outside, looking in, his nose pressed against the glass, pressing so hard the glass broke. And then his silence. The poetry of his silence. Maybe telling her with his silence that he recognized her wild, reckless nature, which couldn't be satisfied with her college crowd.

He thought about the fear and apprehension in her that she so carefully concealed from Chone: he thought about this, and wondered what it was. Maybe it was the upsetting, mysterious threat to her whole view of things that was in Chone's attitude. Here they were on the way to her father and to whatever fate was in store for Chone, and yet Chone made it plain he didn't care what happened; a man acting as if life, not death, awaited him. Or maybe he thought death and life were the two sides of a coin, and he could afford to be indifferent. And look at his bearing! This pool hustler, this gambler's bodyguard, guilty of criminal assaults and God knows what crimes in the past, now had an air of dignity and security. Even the Captain couldn't see through him.

How the hell does he get away with it? he thought. As the ship rolled in the rhythms of the engines, his wonder grew that Chone could believe in his own terrible hold on Gina. The man was astonishing. It was as if Chone had had one of those ancient flashes of illumination that told him he didn't have to care now about hell or high water, or Rosso, or U-boats. This crazy faith! Where did he get it? Where does anyone get it? Out of the depths of his own being? The right reading of some signs? And now Chone, in his new-found faith that he was right and had seen the ultimate pattern of things, had a kind of criminal grandeur. Gina would feel it in his presence; gradually he might begin to make her feel uncertain about everything.

While his concern for Gina grew he did not notice that he was thinking of Chone with a grudging, wondering admiration. Then a little voice coming out of the back of his mind said:

"Ira, my boy, if you don't marry Julia, I think I will." Leo Cawthra! Sure. But why this? And Cawthra! He did remember Leo saying this. After a London air raid they had been in an amateur brothel, and while four girls sat around in a little circle in a plain room with some kind of worn oilcloth on the floor, listening with stunned expressions, he and Leo drunkenly recited "The Shooting of Dan McGrew" with appropriate gestures and

123

got neither applause nor laughter from the earnest little whores. Leo said, "Our ballads aren't right for this country, my friend," and, standing up, went into a mincing recitation of Shelley's "Ode to a Skylark". On and on he went, his eyes closed in ecstasy while the sullen girls glowered, until the buxom amateur madam got their caps, clamped them on their heads, and, taking them in her heavy bare freckled arms, led them to the door and threw them out. It was raining. They walked arm-in-arm in the rain till Leo, still reciting, stopped suddenly, one foot in a puddle, and said gravely,

"The first time I saw Julia, I said to myself, 'Who's the girl with the grin?' Yeah, I remember. Well, Ira, my boy, if you don't marry that girl, I think I will."

"To hell with this," he said, swinging himself out of the bunk. Pulling on his sea boots, he went on deck. The night sky was clearing. When heavy clouds broke away there was a glimpse of the moon, like a naked bulb in a patch of ink, a full moon again silvering the ship. A voice on the bridge made him turn. He could make out the figures there, the Captain moving to the radar cabin. Going aft slowly, he finally stopped near the depth charges where he had stood in the fog with Gina, then coming along by the port rail he suddenly stopped — as if his mind had gone on working at the thing, and he stood fascinated.

"He'll be killed," she had said quietly. Now he thought he saw what she was up to, being so nice, so agreeable, so cosy with Chone, and why she didn't want him to say anything to Chone. She didn't want to say or do anything to weaken his confidence, anything that would make him reflect and turn and run.

Now I know what she's afraid of, he thought. The one thing she had been afraid of all along — that after they had made the crossing and landed, Chone would come to his senses, put her on the way to her father, then run. Run for his life — and keep on running and escape her. Nothing she could do would be too humiliating if it fed Chone's confidence in his domination over her, kept him feeling sure of himself, and enabled her to carry him with her right to the end — where she could turn him in. And it was working for her. She was handling Chone. Gripping the rail and staring at the water in wonder, he thought, Chone is really her prisoner.

And yet something about it bothered him. Why did she

seem so tormented, holding onto my arm, he asked himself. This hidden torment that seemed to have something to do with him — what was it? Did she know herself what it was? Recognizing as she did the absolute necessity of Chone's death as the only thing that could satisfy her pride and give her back her view of herself, she had shown by her emotion how shaken she was — shaken by the terrible necessity. So she was not only in constant fear of Chone running and getting away from her, she must also be afraid of herself and what she might do. And she keeps one hand on me, wanting to be with me, he thought. "Be with me, Ira. Be with me," while her passion drove her to the things that would keep Chone bound to her. And Chone? What would he care what bound him to her, as long as they were bound? And then with sudden anguish he thought, how do I know what really goes on between them?

SIXTEEN

With the U-boat on the horizon, the very quiet tension growing in everyone was not like a nervousness, but more like a grave readiness. Any kind of horseplay among the hands was now irrelevant. Night was coming on after another quiet, monotonous day, and he was in the wardroom sitting in the Captain's place at the end of the little table, eating by himself. The navigator was at the desk writing a letter. As the rattle of dishes came from the nearby galley, Chone came in.

"Gentlemen," he said with the little bow of a headwaiter, and sat down at the table. It could have been in his own place. But why not? He was the Captain's financial friend — the

126

Captain's contact with the world of celebrities who was welcome on the bridge at any time if the Captain was there, which meant he was nearly always on the bridge. Face to face as they were, Chone's self-assurance suddenly riled him, and he tried to meet his eyes.

"Sausages and tomatoes again, Mr. Chone," he said. "I imagine you'll be glad to get ashore."

"Stewed tomatoes? Good," Chone said. "You know, when I was a kid, I used to love stewed tomatoes."

"You loved stewed tomatoes?"

"I did."

"When you were a kid. Where was that?"

"Brooklyn."

"Well, now you can feel you're back home. By the way, I notice you watching the water a lot. Are you worried?"

"Not at all. It's a habit you get into on this ship. Everybody does it, so now I do it. They tell me to look for something like the periscope's little white feather running along the surface. Right?"

"Right — if the U-boat's in the convoy."

"I'm betting it is."

"Is Miss Bixby worried?"

"Not while she's with me. No."

"No, of course not," he said, an edge on his voice.

"Everything depends on the way a man feels," Chone said calmly. "And I figure they've taken their best shot at me." Then, hesitating, he dropped his maddening air of security; he had a sudden gentle dignity.

"Could I say something personal, sir?"

"Go ahead, Mr. Chone."

"I very much appreciate the way you've all made Miss Bixby feel so safe and at ease. A girl in her situation could feel so out of place here, she'd want to hide. But there's been," and he hesitated to get the right careful words, "warm informality. Yeah, that's it. Warm informality. I appreciate it. She appreciates it too, sir. And I would like to think we could extend our hospitality to you . . . when we get ashore, and are in London. I'd like you to have a fine hotel dinner with us, a change from this fare. A grand dinner with all the wines — if you could be in London."

"If I could be in London?"

127

"That's right."

"You'll be there with Miss Bixby?"

"Of course I will."

"Well now," he fumbled his words awkwardly, feeling his way, "How would you get in touch with me, Mr. Chone?"

"I'll leave word with the American Express Company — telling how you can get in touch with us. Okay?"

"I see," he said, surprised by Chone's genuine, massive certainty that he was in no trouble. Chone obviously did not dream of running when he got ashore. So Gina had him! She had him bound hand and foot, and now Chone's calm, arrogant assurance suddenly seemed so pitiable that he wanted to say to him, "You silly, unaware, cocksure bastard, if you get ashore, run for your life from her." Then, as their eyes met, he knew Chone wouldn't believe in the fate that was in store for him. He would be amused. And even here, their eyes meeting, Chone gave off a sense of certainty about his own power. It was in his solid shoulders, in the set of his head.

"He wasn't always like this," Gina had said. So his sense of power had come after he had nursed his passion, hanging around Gina, nursed his suffering, too. He had done something about it. He had taken her. And the power had come to him from the thing he had done, as if he knew he had reached the core of her being, and he thought now she knew it, too, and so he was sure everything would fall into place for them. Everything had meaning now. Staring in wonder at Chone, Groome couldn't speak. Then some grim satisfaction must have shown in his own face as he thought, how blind he is! For Chone, in his turn, looked at him with sudden, wary surprise.

The navigator, who had finished his letter, left the desk and came over with his warm, available wide-mouthed grin,

"I think I'll join you for a drink," he said.

"And I must be on my way," he said abruptly. But as he left he felt a little chill and turned. Chone, his eyes full of new, hard appraisal, said, "You've got the cold hand, Mr. Groome."

"What?"

"Archeology, my ass. You're a gravedigger."

"Not yours, Mr. Chone," and he left. He was sure Chone would get rid of him — if he had to. Somehow Chone would get rid of him. He was glad they were still on the ship. He thought:

why, the arrogant son of a bitch! One little word out of him on this ship — one little gesture that's out of line and I'll throw him in the brig and keep him there, and if he has anything to say about it when we get ashore he'll see how tough I can get.

SEVENTEEN

And with sunlight gone and the horizon creeping in, the
ships riding in the convoy became faint fading shadows, and
when the real dark came and no stars appeared, it got cold. The
sky, the air, the sea, became one thick, black, cold, murky wet
blanket wrapped around them and freezing the skin under their
duffle coats. Nothing seemed to move any more; it was like
when you wake up in bed at night and there is no light in the
room at all.

When he was on his way to the bridge the Yorkshireman
approached him in a dignified, formal manner.

"Could I have a word with you, sir?"

"What's up?"

"Well sir, I have a special and useful talent. I'm a machinist."

"All right. A machinist. So what?"

"I was wondering if I could help in some way. Everybody has been good to me. Can't I help, sir?"

"All right. Thanks. I told you to see the bosun," he said, slapping him on the shoulder.

On the bridge where the Captain kept raising his glasses, Ira Groome would stare into the black, soupy night, telling himself he had wonderful eyes and could still see the water. A little breeze came up, at first in puffs, then steadily, icily, heavily, yet without clearing the air. It was the coldest night of the crossing. He moved over by the Oerlikon gun. He could see the shape of the navigator's head, the light from the binnacle lamp making a little patch of light on his face, and in this light the navigator seemed to have no body. There was also a little strip of light coming from the asdic hut. No one on the bridge moved in the cold, silent darkness.

About an hour before dawn, when they were a little way off from the convoy, a distress rocket shooting up well to starboard made a sudden unbelievable rush of fire across the blanket of the night.

"There it is. They've got her," the Captain said.

"Far over on the starboard wing," he said, watching where the sky was bright with criss-crossing rockets shooting high, then quickly fading. No signal came from the asdic operator to indicate he had a contact. Off to port, a ship began to burn with a stab of orange flame that bellied out brightly, the flames hanging there in the night.

Then the asdic operator called sharply, "The contact's so faint, sir. The U-boat may be on the surface."

The rattle sounded; the ship was suddenly alive with the men closing at the action stations. Then he noticed with surprise that Chone had come up to the bridge, as he did every day, as the Captain in the beginning had invited him to do, and he was keeping well out of the way at the corner of the ladder.

"Can you give us a bearing?" the Captain asked the operator.

"About thirty degrees off the port bow, sir." The Captain went into the asdic hut, he followed, and there they estimated that the U-boat was about seven hundred yards ahead, thirty degrees off the port bow.

"The star shells, No. 1," the Captain said. He called quietly down to the gun crew, "Bearing red 30, 700 yards."

"Bearing red 30, 700 yards," came the answer, and the four-inch gun swung into position. The voices were clear but quiet.

"Star shell, star shell, star shell," he called. "Commence, commence, commence."

The first star shell swished up like a beautiful Roman candle, and as it descended it hung there momentarily, and the bright glowing reflection became a golden bowl of light on the polished ebony water; the bowl got smaller and smaller, then it was gone, and the paths of light that led to it were blotted out. The gun crew fired four rounds. On the fourth round the star shell opened up beautifully, the long, shimmering paths of light led to the beautiful golden bowl. Then he saw it; he really saw it. It looked like a black beetle crawling into the golden bowl, and he cried out in astonishment. "I saw it!" No one paid any attention to him. "That got it. I saw it," he yelled.

"Are you sure, No. 1?" the Captain asked.

"Lighted up like a big bug," he said. "It was perfect. I saw it."

"Where?"

"Right there!"

"I don't see anything," the Captain said, his glasses trained on that one spot in the water. "Keep looking, sir," he said quietly to the Captain, as if he were giving the orders. "Keep looking, sir," he repeated.

His sense of expectancy was now so unbearable he couldn't force his eyes to focus on that one area. The Captain, after staring at him, swung around quickly to the asdic hut. "Have you got it?" he called to the operator.

"I — I had it, sir," the operator yelled.

"What do you mean you had it?"

In the hut's patch of light the operator, without answering, kept listening, angry determination plain on his face.

"I — I've lost it," he said, his voice trembling with excitement.

"But did you have it?"

"I'm sure I had it, sir."

"Maybe you were right, No. 1," the Captain said. "I don't know. Everybody's a little excited."

"It could have dived, sir."

"It could have. Yes."

"That means it's in the convoy."

"That's what it would mean — if you really saw it."

"But I saw it plainly, sir."

"Well, maybe you did," and he knew the Captain didn't believe him. The U-boat had been there plainly, held in the light as it might never be seen again, yet he felt an incredible doubt of himself, as though the thing he had seen might not actually have been there in the water but only in his own mind, like the apparition, the vivid mirage, the table with the one empty chair.

"I'll believe my own eyes," he thought grimly, and he stayed on the bridge, while the mist got lighter and thinner, till there was a faint gray streak on the horizon.

"I've got it again, sir," the operator yelled.

"Where is it?" the Captain asked, very quiet and unruffled; he had to be convinced. In the light from the asdic hut the expressions on all their faces could be seen. The Captain, who looked very solid and unexcited, smiled, knowing the operator was doggedly determined his Captain should be convinced it was the real thing this time.

"Closer than before," the operator called, and then there was only the sound of the operator's voice as they plotted the path of the submarine.

"Bearing 035, 2250 yards," then an unendurable silence till the voice came again. "Bearing 030, 1500 yards." More silence, then "Bearing 030, 750 yards." The tightening knot in his stomach changed to a catch in his throat as he took over the gun. It was very quiet on the bridge.

Months of heightened expectancy seemed to have brought him to this place, and now he felt elated; he heard the Captain alter his course until they were only two hundred yards off.

"Stand by for the depth charges," the Captain said in such a casual tone that he turned, looked at him in surprise, and waited in an inexplicable gap in the action, a long, meaningless wait, for the Captain to give the order to drop the pattern of depth charges. Actually they only waited a few seconds.

"Attack with the depth charges," the Captain said. You

could hear the depth charges plop, plop into the water as the ship slid along; then came the muffled blasts, and the pattern of geyser sprays on the water while the ship rolled, shivered, then slid along evenly. Still at the gun, he ordered the signalman to mark with flares the position where they had dropped their charges. By this time they were going hard to port trying to pick up the sub's echo, and he had the Oerlikon gun turned on the bearing of the flares as the quiet voices of the lookouts came to him.

"Flare red 110, flare red 70, flare red 40." Then the contact again as they steadied their course, going into the attack just as it got a little brighter, light enough for them to see a peculiar wake appearing on the water, a wake that hadn't been made by the ship. But there really was no time to notice it. It was just one of the things coming at him very fast, till the U-boat suddenly swooshed up, with water sliding off it in the dawn light. There it was, only two hundred yards away.

"Submarine on the surface," he called to the Captain. He had kept his voice so quiet and casual that the tone fooled the Captain, who came leaping to his side of the bridge, an irritated expression on his face.

"Are you still seeing things, No. 1 — by Jove," and he stopped, full of vast surprise.

"There she is," he said.

"Look. The conning tower."

"They'll go for their gun."

"Easy, No. 1."

The surfaced U-boat was there, and he could see crewmen clawing their way up from the conning tower. They came stumbling up drunkenly, some of them lurching their way aft; three of them, grabbing at the guns, tried to get them into position.

"Will I open fire, sir?" he asked. His own Oerlikon was trained on the figures that milled around on the U-boat's deck, trying to train their gun on the ship's bridge, on him. Those figures out there were getting ready to kill him off, he thought. Just two hundred yards away, half-hidden in the thin light, death waited for him among the ridiculous dancing figures framed against the choppy waves; their arms looked so tiny, grabbing at the gun, that the thought of death advancing toward him in that cold light filled him with surprise.

134

"Carry on, No. 1," he heard the Captain say, and he fired a burst. He wanted to keep them from coming up from the conning tower. At least two of the figures that had been dancing along the foothold toppled into the water. All the figures looked very small and ridiculous jumping around in a row with the vast, unending stretch of water as a backdrop. Then the U-boat opened fire. The burst swept the length of the ship, and even while he kept on firing at the dancing figures, he was aware of the signalman sitting down very slowly, blood spurting from his shoulder as he smiled stupidly, tried to get up, touched the shoulder, saw the smear of blood on his hand, looked awfully surprised, and then rolled over on his face. The air reeked of cordite; the empty shell cases rattling on the steel bridge rolled around wildly, and four more of the little figures near the U-boat gun toppled into the water. Then he heard the voice of Chone, who had been standing out of the way at the rail near the ladder, and who now had moved out, and who was laughing and shouting:

"Blow the heads off the two-bit sons of bitches."

"What?" the Captain said. Then he yelled, "Get the hell off my bridge, Mr. Chone."

"Yes, sir," Chone said, and hurried down the ladder. He had heard Chone, he had heard the Captain, but his eyes remained on the men coming up from the conning tower, who milled helplessly around their gun. They were backing away from it, waving their hands. They kept dancing around, keeping their hands up.

"Are they quitting?" the Captain shouted. "Yes, they're quitting. Hold your fire, No. 1."

"Why would they quit like that, sir?" he yelled. "Maybe the depth charges — "

The U-boat crew were backing away from their gun. It could have been knocked out; they were signalling surrender and his whole being was filled with elation.

"I want a couple of prisoners," the Captain said. "Their skipper and their engineer. And their logbooks and code books, any official-looking papers. How would you like to board her, No. 1?"

"Very much, sir."

"If their gun is all right they could blow a boat out of the water. Well, I'm closing on her and keeping our big gun trained on them. A single move toward their gun and I'll blow them out of the water. Go ahead. Give the order for a boarding party. And don't worry. We'll cover you."

Five of the crew got into the boat with him: an engineer who would be needed to look at the sub's engines, a stoker, Horler the bosun, leading seamen Henderson, and Frawley, the wiry, swarthy boy who had been a plumber's assistant on the west coast.

Just before the boat was lowered he looked up and saw Gina and Chone, who were keeping well out of the way, Chone holding her arm. And she had on the mauve coat she had been wearing the day they had picked her up. It seemed important to notice this coat and wonder where they could put her now that the wounded signalman had been taken to the sick bay. In that quick moment, in that one glance as he got into the boat, he saw that Chone's eyes were on him, on him alone; no excitement at all in Chone's demeanor, just solid, secure, and thoughtful contemplation of him, as if he knew what was going to happen to him — as if he knew they were seeing each other for the last time. It was a bad feeling to have just as the boat was being lowered. In the excitement the boat was lowered too rapidly, and when it hit the water it shot off at such a crazy angle they were all sure it would capsize; yet they got it righted.

EIGHTEEN

Then he turned and looked into the faces of his own men who, with their heavy sea boots on, wouldn't have much chance in the water. Then he looked over at the U-boat. Some of their crew were launching their own rubber boat.

"Now take it easy," he said. "Nice and easy, our big gun is trained on that U-boat. One false move out of them and Horler'll use the Sten gun. Nice and easy, Horler. Nice and easy does it." On the U-boat six men with their hands up waited near the conning tower.

As the boat dipped and rose in the choppy sea and he tried to make out those faces near the conning tower, his stomach contracted because the sweep of the oars taking the boat closer seemed to be such a very purposeful, too purposeful, rhythmic motion on that gray sea with its too choppy, broken little waves, and he watched the six on the U-boat near the conning tower, who remained motionless, their hands still up.

"Your captain," he shouted as the boat came alongside. "I want your captain." But no one on the U-boat answered. They just waited, keeping their hands up.

"Your captain — your engineer," he shouted again, and as if they half understood now, they pointed at their own gun, then over the water at the corvette's gun. Maybe they were saying their captain had been killed. In their rocking boat, the seamen stared at the enemy, who watched them silently.

"Come on. We're going aboard, Horler," he said. He climbed aboard with Horler and his gun, and the engineer and the stoker. With Horler following, he went as far as halfway between the conning tower and the stern, where he stopped, facing the crew.

"Goddamn it, someone speaks English," he shouted, and felt tough and angry. He ordered one of them into the ship's boat. He had to point at the boat. They didn't understand him. He had half expected the enemy to be fanatical or dramatic; instead they seemed to be petrified, just a little group of frightened men, and he hadn't even taken his gun from his holster. He grabbed the one nearest to him, a small man, and pointed to the conning tower. The little man wouldn't move. He gave him a violent push. The little man lurched around as if too frightened to obey, and suddenly this too looked all wrong. It was like watching a movie, knowing something bad had to happen, and it would be wrong if it didn't happen. He pushed the small man roughly toward the conning tower, paying no attention to his jabbering protests and desperate pleas.

The little man's hand came out, and then, as if afraid the gesture might be misunderstood, he withdrew the hand and shook his head hysterically.

"Do I have to blow your head off?" he shouted, putting his hand on his own gun. Then, shoving him aside in disgust, he climbed up the conning tower and looked down. Something's going to happen, he thought; and his anxiety was so painful, it made him feel he knew this was the place where it was to happen.

138

After looking down into the conning tower, he turned to his own men, who had the prisoners herded into a group. Horler's Sten gun was trained on the group, and the wide gray sea rose around them, and the wet narrow deck was just a sliver on the vastness of the sea.

"Keep it just like this," he shouted to Horler. "One false move and use the gun, Horler." Just before he went down the conning tower he took another look at the man he had shoved, who seemed to be frozen in bewilderment. Then, as he lowered himself into the darkness, he tightened up; he was sweating, yet he felt himself being drawn down. He had the flashlight in his left hand and he paused, using it. No movement down there, quiet and dark as the grave down there. Where should he begin his search for the U-boat's papers? Before continuing his descent, he looked back up at the patch of gray friendly light that seemed to be beckoning urgently, and then there was a loud crash. The whole U-boat shook, and he started climbing fast.

When his head rose above the conning tower level he saw his men jumping into the water and swimming toward their boat. The conning tower now was only a few feet out of the water, with the U-boat going down stern first, the water closing in ever so slowly and gently in little soft gray folds, then creeping up at the conning tower. He crawled out of the conning tower, looking aft for Horler, the engineer, and the stoker, who were in the water about fifteen feet away. Their heads bobbed in the water as they swam for their boat, where Henderson leaned over the side. The water, creeping over the U-boat deck and rising slowly around the conning tower, rose, too, around that one man who had had the frightened, frantic air, and who still stood looking bewildered as they gaped at each other. This man was the enemy. He had never been face to face with the enemy. The little man, yelling something, came a step closer, one hand thrust out, the other one waving wildly. Thinking the man was going to hit him, he backed away, then swung at him blindly. Yet even as he swung he half tried to stop the blow, realizing that the man was out of his mind, but his fist, catching him on the jaw, toppled the man into the water, which by this time was sucking the U-boat down.

He stood there stupidly, looking at his flashlight, then he clutched at the little ladder on the conning tower, climbed up three steps, freeing himself from the sucking water, while the men in the boat yelled at him, then he turned and dived, getting as much propulsion from the ladder as he could for the long, arching dive, and then he came up, and he was swimming hard and frantically toward the boat to get away from the suction of the sinking sub that was pulling at him.

The U-boat went down neatly just as if it were diving, then there was only one wake on the water, and while the wake widened there was a rolling, muffled roar, sounding like an explosion of a depth charge, and it made the boat roll and rock. A gray geyser of water shooting into the air lifted the boat, overturned it, and tossed them into the water. He came up, choking, and saw heads bobbing up in a widening circle, all the heads slowly moving toward the overturned boat. He reached it first. He clawed at the boat, using all his strength to help right it. A wave slapped at his face; he was tired after the jump from the tower and the swim to the boat; his heavy sea boots were sucking him down.

Now the boat was circling crazily away from them like a chip on a whirlpool. The explosion, lifting the sub again in the water, had created a new, more powerful suction that was spinning the boat and sucking it down, and he went down too, till the lifebelt thrust him up. Down again he went, again he bobbed up, then he felt himself being pulled and held down, and he clawed at his heavy sea boots, clawing at them, kicking out desperately, frightened by his bursting chest, and the utter blackness of his mind. Then came bright flashes in the darkness, the last flashes of life at the end, and the words: "Who are my father and mother? What is my name?" as if it was all that had to be known now, all that was really important, this personal identification. It was absolutely necessary now, if he was entering into death, to know who he was and where he came from, and then one more flash in the darkness: his mother's face, and a lilac tree growing in their garden.

But his head shot up above the surface. Hands grabbed at his hair, and, hanging loosely in the water, he was being pulled into the boat, gasping for breath, and for a minute or two he was lying with his head in someone's lap. Then he said, "The boat. Was it thrown up right?" and he really came to his senses and sat up. He watched one of the hands, still in the water, being pulled away from them, no matter how hard he swam.

"Horler," he shrieked like a cheer leader, "you can do it, Horler." Bit by bit Horler came closer, then close enough so Groome could lunge over the side and get him by the hand and haul him in and hug him.

Shouts still came from the water where the U-boat men, whose own rubber boat had been upturned by the explosion, were swimming after the ship's boat. The men, who had been rowing, stopped and looked back as the first of the swimmers reached the boat and a hand came up over the stern, a brown, wet hand. Horler asked, "What do we do, sir? No room here, sir." Henderson said, "What the hell. Let them get to their own float and look after it." Horler said, "We can't take them in this boat, right, sir?" Yet he hesitated, his eyes on the wet hand that had reached up, reached up to him, reached into him: and then Horler was saying with his eyes, "What's the matter with you? It's them or us. They're not really us. Come on."

So he said to the stoker, "Knock the hand off. It's tough. But this is the way it is," and the stoker knocked the hand loose, and they watched the swimmer fall back with his own struggling comrades, stringing out one by one in a lengthening, broken trail of water. And in the boat the rowers, facing them, had to watch their arms come up and go down, and listen to their terrible lonely cries. No one said anything till they got close to their ship and could see the excited faces of their comrades and hear them cheering. Everybody was laughing . They were all laughing and pointing at him standing in the boat. Only then did he realize he had lost his pants as well as the sea boots.

After the boat had been raised and there was a lot of hand-shaking and backslapping and joking, he saw Chone, still with Gina, beyond the group at the rail. In Chone's face there was no trace of chagrin or frustration at seeing him unharmed. As their eyes met, Chone bowed; then, grinning indulgently, he clapped his hands slowly, very slowly, in lordly applause.

NINETEEN ≋≋≋≋≋≋≋≋≋≋≋≋≋≋≋≋

On deck it was like a holiday afternoon with the sun shining, the ships in convoy moving along in their lanes and the sea sparkling; and he was wearing his best suit of clothes. None of the hands slept. They came up from the lower deck to relax and enjoy themselves and listen to Horler. Everybody was a little drunk with pride, and he promenaded on the deck in his good clothes, feeling at ease with everyone. Gina and Chone came up to him.

"Congratulations," she called, and he noticed that her arm was under Chone's. It was the first time he had seen her holding Chone's arm. It was as if she was sure now they would land, and this was the way she would go ashore.

"You scared the wits out of me, Lieutenant," she said. In Chone's presence she was not calling him Ira.

"It went very well," he said.

"You've got a good right hand," Chone said, grinning. "That was a beautiful swing."

"I don't think I should have hit him at all."

"If a man's got a punch like that, he's got to use it. Why not use it?"

"Well, I think now he was hysterical."

"But how do you know?"

"Well, I don't know. I suppose."

"That's it. You don't know."

"Do you know they've thrown me out of the sick bay?" Gina asked, smiling. "The wounded boy is there now."

"What do you do, Miss Bixby? Sleep on the deck?"

"No. She changes place with me," Chone said. "The Captain's cabin for her. A hammock somewhere for me."

"It's only to be for a day or two anyway now," she said. Then, hesitating, her tone changing, "Mr. Groome — "

"Yes?"

"Out there, you must have thought you were drowning . . . I seemed to feel you thinking it . . . I don't know . . . "

"Yes, it's a funny thing — " he said awkwardly. "Going down, things come very fast. Pictures flash in your mind. Well, it's a cliché but, dammit, they do. Going down again — in the blackness I saw the lilac tree, all blooming in the garden at home."

"Not the Yucatan? Home?" she asked.

"That's right. Home," and he turned to Chone. "Mr. Chone, I saw you on the bridge — under fire. What got into you?"

"What got into me?" he repeated, taken aback, then reaching for a little joke. "I know a man in New York who'd know just what to say."

"A man in New York."

"A little man with built-up shoes. Name of Willard Arp."

"What would he say?"

"He'd say I got stage-struck," and he laughed heartily. "Yeah, that's the great thing," he said. "To be stage-struck in the right way, at the right time. Come on, Gina," and they went along the deck. Looking over her shoulder when she was ten steps away, she glanced back at him while she went off with Chone. He didn't see them again the rest of the day. After dinner the exhaustion he had been ignoring all day overwhelmed him. In the cabin he lay flat on his back, his feet about sixteen inches apart, his hands linked behind his head, listening to the ticking of his wrist watch, then to the familiar little noises, the squeaks, the sway of the ship, the wailing of the engine-room pump, peaceful sounds soothing him, and sleep came easily.

And then in his sleep his whole body began to shake to a clanging rattle. Rolling himself to the side of the couch and swinging his feet out, he began inflating his lifebelt. Then came the roaring blast. The side of the built-in couch caved in, toppled him, threw him out, smacked him against the torn door jamb, and threw him hard against broken, jagged splinters from the post. Blood streamed down his wrist and all over his hand. The ship vibrated like a twanged taut cord, and he heard yelling and the pounding of feet.

Stunned, he lay there till the pounding and the roar beating in on him hurt his head. His eyes opened, but in the dark he couldn't see anything. He felt around, finding long splinters of wood near him and a broken board which he pushed away. All around him was a whirl of rushing sounds. Shouts got louder, then faded. In the pitch dark his mind began to clear a little, he wondered irrelevantly what time it was, and tried to get up. He couldn't. An excruciating pain shot through his arm. Blood was dripping down the arm. In the dark he could feel the warm blood in his hand. Groping around, he found his duffle coat, dragged it on, and stumbling to the ladder he hoisted himself up painfully. Halfway up, he turned and looked back, as if he had forgotten something.

On deck there was moonlight, bright moonlight, and he looked up at the bridge, expecting to see the Captain shouting instructions. No one was there. The ship was settling at the stern. The deck was sloping, and shouts were coming from the port side where hands who had not got into lowered boats were jumping into the water.

He staggered toward the bridge ladder, and had taken three steps up the ladder before his mind cleared. He backed down and then saw someone lying by the rail: the Captain, his neck twisted. Dead. Hurled down the ladder at the deck, he thought. So he wouldn't be going home to face a still-too-beautiful wife. No such problems for the Captain.

He couldn't see anyone else on the deck, which meant that the boats had been lowered, and he was there alone in the moonlight, and no one knew he was there. And no one knew Gina was in the sick bay; he made his way there. Then he remembered. The signalman, not Gina, had been there, and the signalman was gone. Cries came from the water. He got to the rail and saw three hands sliding on the ropes, and down there in the black water, heads bobbing around a boat they were righting. A voice came from the water: it sounded like Horler:

"Swim out men, or you'll be sucked down when she sinks. Swim out and the boats will pick you up. Keep that boat moving out. That's it." But then a belch of smoke came rolling toward him, he was lost in it as he crawled to the port side to the place where the lifeboat had been. Ropes hung down to the water; but down there, no boat. Just faces. Or he thought he saw faces. In the fine clear moonlight he could see faces. The boys on the ropes could have jumped away from the ship so they would not swing hard against the side. While he was inflating his lifebelt, he saw a large object, a float, sweeping toward the ship, then sweeping away, rocking and sweeping. And then he heard a woman's scream. Keeping his eyes on this float, he jumped, flopping through the air, and his body smacked against the water.

His lifebelt brought him up to the surface, but he was choking in some oil; oil that could get into his eyes and throat and blind him and choke him and weigh him down. He heard someone calling "Here".

"Help, help," he cried, clawing his way out of the patch of oil. "Help, help." An object in the water bumped against him. A body, sitting in the water. It came floating against him, the head lolling back lifelessly: a bearded face. The oil getting into the Yorkshireman's beautiful beard had helped to choke him.

"Here," he heard the yell again, only now it sounded fainter and far away.

"Here," he gasped.

"Here, here," the faraway voice answered, and he dragged himself through the water with a heavy ploughing motion, using

145

one arm, and he knew he would be all right now, and in the moonlight he could clearly see other men who floated around and yelled wildly, their arms shooting up so they could be seen and picked up. Then the float, lifted high on a wave, came sliding down to him and he clawed at the ropes.

His weight tilted the light float toward him and someone, grabbing his wrist, pulled him in and rolled him over the thick rounded rim.

"Yeah, it's No.1 all right," the voice said. "Come on, No.1."

"Yeah — " he gasped. "Boseley — "

"Boseley, yeah."

"I'm all right, Boseley," and then he was looking up in their faces bending down close to his. Boseley's round sullen face and Mason, the sick-bay attendant.

Mason had blood on his hand and he held it up and looked at it. "Must be coming from your arm," he said. While Mason was opening his duffle coat, getting at the arm, he closed his eyes and gradually got his breath and some strength. Then he saw Gina at the end of the float, huddled up in a duffle coat, clutching the ropes on the float. In the bright moonlight she sat stunned and staring, as if she could not comprehend why this, which had happened to her before, should actually be happening again.

"No," she kept saying dully. "No, no," and stared and saw nothing.

"Gina," he called. "Gina." She didn't answer. "How did she get here?" he asked.

"I got her out of the Captain's cabin," Mason said.

"You're great, Mason."

"I'm the sick-bay attendant. No boat for us. It wasn't there. I got a rope around her."

"I got the rope," said Boseley, busy with his paddle.

"So you did, Boseley."

"You bet I did."

Having pulled the sweater sleeve high on the bleeding arm, Mason's own hands now dripped blood. "It's awful. Seems to be a vein on the underside of your arm," he said. "A wood splinter got into you. You'll bleed to death. Well, here goes," and opening his own duffle coat, Mason pulled the belt from his pants, looped it tightly around the arm just above the elbow, forced a new hole in the leather, and buckled the belt into a tourniquet.

"There," he said. "In a little while you'll have to loosen that, sir. That's what I understand, anyway. I'm no doctor," and after dipping his own bloody hands over the rim of the float, he put the arm back in the duffle-coat sleeve.

"Gina," he said. "Gina," and she half turned in a stupor. She began to shiver. She looked around wildly at the ship, the sky, and the water, and then at the water again, where it was as bright as day and where heads bobbed up and men cried out as they swam toward the ship's boat now a hundred feet away. Another float with six men on it was further away.

"Gina, are you all right?" he called as he hunched his body closer to her. "Gina — "

"Eh?" she said vaguely, without turning from the water. Suddenly she gripped his good hand in a fierce, nervous grip and half stood up.

"Jesus, lady, don't," shouted Boseley, who was trying to paddle the float away from the ship's side.

"There he is," she yelled wildly, pointing up at the ship's rail. In the bright moonlight they could see a figure half-draped over the rail, the figure very plain to see in that light and maybe she recognized the hunched-up heavy shoulders.

"Jethroe, Jethroe," she screamed. "Jethroe." But his head still hung over the rail. Turning, she cried, "Ira — don't you leave him there. Get him down, Ira. Goddamn it. Get him down."

"Jump, Chone, jump," Boseley yelled.

"Jump," he too yelled. "We'll get you." Up there on the rail Chone raised his head slowly as if gathering himself together, then the heavy figure came rolling slowly over the rail, it rolled out of the deck moonlight into the shadow of the ship's side, then flopped into the water not more than ten feet away, where his inflated lifebelt held him up. Boseley paddled the float toward him. Both Mason and Boseley grabbed at him. One got him by the hair, another by the shoulder, and they rolled him in over the rim of the tilting float onto the webbing floor, where he lay with his eyes closed.

"Get this float away from the ship," he ordered them. "Get away fast. Come on. We'll be sucked in when she goes down. The float will tip." With Boseley paddling hard, they did begin to move slowly away from the ship, then he looked at Chone who was lying at the end of the float near Mason, who was talking to him.

"Mr. Chone, Mr. Chone, can you hear me?"

"Sure," he said.

"Where are you hurt?"

"My side. My whole side feels caved in."

"What happened?"

"I was asleep. Bang!" He couldn't get his breath. The pain made him wince. Then he went on. "I'm thrown out of the hammock hard against something big and heavy," he gasped.

Mason, who had been feeling under Chone's duffle coat, shook his head and looked at his hand. No blood on his hand. And then he put the hand on Chone's mouth. Then a little trickle of blood came from the corner of Chone's mouth, a little dark line down to his chin in the moonlight.

"Must be bleeding internally," Mason said. "I can't do anything. Maybe he could hemorrhage. I don't know. Just pray to God he doesn't. I don't know what to do."

"Jethroe," Gina called, and she went crawling closer to Chone. "Jethroe," she said softly.

Raising his head, he asked, "You're all right, aren't you Gina?"

"I'm all right. Not hurt at all."

"Ah, you see. Ah," and he grinned. In that light the grin looked crazy. Lifting himself a little more, till his shoulder could rest on the rim of the float where the moonlight was on his big bearded face, he jerked his head back, and he had all his sense of certainty. "The sons of bitches keep on trying, don't they, Gina?" he said, still grinning. "Yet you're all right, and I'm here too. You see, what did I tell you? This is rotten, but you're all right and we're here and we'll soon be picked up."

"You bet," she said, "And we'll be on our way again," and she came crawling back to her place. "Yeah, Ira, there he is," she said grimly as she leaned closer. "Look at him, Ira," and he didn't know whether there was bitter mockery in her tone, or wonder. Or even some terrible satisfaction. For when she had cried out so commandingly, "Goddamn it. Get him down," he had been shaken by her tone. Was it that even now Jethroe Chone was not to be allowed to get away? If so, why did she move him so deeply now?

"We've only got this damned paddle," Boseley shouted. It was a short paddle and he couldn't do much with it.

There was a screen of webbing in the bottom of the float, but their feet lay in water, and as he looked around, the first thing he noticed was his own foot against Gina's; her other foot touched Boseley's, whose own foot touched Mason's; all the feet in the middle of the float. And no foot near Chone's.

"Try and get us away from the ship, Boseley," he yelled. "It's sinking. For Christ's sake, paddle. Paddle like hell!" and he watched the corvette which seemed to hover on the water, the stern going down slowly. While Boseley paddled frantically, Mason flailed at the water with his hand. As the float slid a little further away from the ship, his own good hand, hanging over the side, hit something; he pulled the thing closer. It was Henderson, the leading seaman. He let him slide away.

"Poor old Henderson, what hit him?" Boseley said, then he yelled, "Look out." The light float, swirling around in the water, was being pulled toward the place where the ship was sinking, sucked in closer, though Boseley paddled desperately against the pull. The float spun around like a top. Then suddenly there was no ship, the float was circling gently, the moon went behind heavy clouds, and in the utter dark, faint voices came from far away.

"She's gone," Boseley said. "What do we do, No.1?"

"Take it easy for a while," he said.

"What time did you say it was, Ira?" she asked quietly.

"I'd say about three."

"What are our chances?"

"Pretty good."

"Supposing there's a bad storm and a very rough sea?"

"We try and hang on."

"Not so good, eh?"

"In the meantime maybe we get picked up."

"Maybe, eh? No maybe about it with Jethroe here. Come on, Ira," and she laughed. She had regained her wonderful control of herself; now he didn't know whether she was being sardonic, or whether, as he had suspected, she was really caught up in the power of Chone's sense of certainty that they were marked out for some other fate ashore. "Jethroe," she called, inching her way to him. "Jethroe . . . "

"How are you, Gina?"

149

"Getting used to things."

"It's still a sure thing, Gina."

"What's a sure thing?"

"That we'll be picked up."

"How do you know?"

"It's not a case of knowing, Gina," he said, speaking slowly now and with great difficulty. "For us this thing just is. No other way to go, Gina."

"Keep it going, Jethroe," she said gently, and held her hand on his forehead.

"Why did you do that, Gina?" Chone asked.

"So we'll all have luck," she said.

"What is this?" Boseley demanded loudly. "Touching a guy's head for luck. I used to play ball, and we had a little black boy for a mascot, and every time I went to bat I used to touch his head, and I led the league in hitting. Is Mr. Chone so lucky, Miss Bixby?"

"Yes, he is," she said.

"So you led the league in hitting, eh Bo?" Mason said. "Like hell. You never got the ball out of the infield."

"Listen, smart guy. Scouts from the big league talked to me."

"What position did you play?" Gina asked.

"The outfield. I was a great natural hitter."

"I'll bet you were. Well, who's going to win the World Series?"

"The Dodgers, Miss Bixby."

"Ever see them play?"

"No, I didn't."

"Look, Boseley," she said. "If you can get to New York, I'll take you to Brooklyn, then I'll take you to dinner."

"No kidding!"

"Is it a deal?"

"Wait a minute. How do I get to New York?"

"I'll give you my address. You write me and come. It'll be a pleasure. Won't it, Jethroe?" and Chone, who lay there so inertly he could have been only half-conscious, said weakly, "Yeah, we'll send you the fare."

"All this on the level?" Boseley asked.

"Strictly on the level," Chone said, his voice a little stron-

150

ger, as if this talk had suddenly buoyed him up. And he too, listening, was buoyed up.

It wasn't so bad here on the float, he told himself. It was a very good place. The float couldn't sink. Up they went on a cresting wave, then down into the troughs. His arm, with the circulation cut off, felt heavy and numb. In a little while, unless they moved, their feet would freeze. In the meantime they could drift around aimlessly; he could wish for the moon to come out again or stars to appear. Instead it started to rain. The steady monotonous gentle rain seemed to make the float smaller, a speck somewhere in the darkness, and for a while no one spoke and he, like the others, except Chone, held on to the ropes.

"How did we get hit?" he asked finally. "I was sleeping."

"It smacked us near the engine room," Boseley said. "Sort of sneaked in on us. The rattle went, then it hit us."

"What happened to our boats?"

"One on the port side banged against the ship's side while it was being lowered, and then tipped."

"Anybody see the U-boat?"

"No one I know of."

"We're going to get out of this," Gina said, her head down. "The things you have to put up with in this world to get anywhere at all. Well, we just put up with it," and then she called "Eh, Jethroe? Hey, Jethroe!" as if bent on keeping him alert and alive. His arm, his hand came up. It was hard to see him in that light, but it looked as if his fist was clenched. "And we make it, Gina," he said.

"Guys do crazy things, don't they?" Boseley said suddenly. "I was standing there, feeling glad I didn't get into the cracked-up boat, then I saw the float. Saying goodbye to the ship, I felt I had to grab at something that belonged to me, and I see Miss Bixby with Mason, and I grab her and put the rope around her."

"Come on, Boseley," he said sharply. "You're with friends." He was taking command of this float. His weakness was from the loss of blood. The pain in his shoulder came from the growing numbness in his arm where the tourniquet cut off the circulation. But his head was clear. "If we stay around till dawn, someone will see us. So just take it easy. The thing to do is to keep warm." It was too dark for him to see whether Chone still had that trickle of blood at his mouth. Only Chone knew how badly he was hurt. He had shifted his body so that even in the dark his eyes would be on Gina; he might be waiting for it to get light enough so that she could see that his eyes were on her.

Involuntarily they all drew closer together, seeking some warmth; all but Chone, who now seemed further away from them. In the silence, he thought he heard Mason praying. As for himself, he tried to believe this was not the place marked out for his death. It kept raining. Since there was little wind, it was just softly falling rain, caressing them in the darkness. Then it stopped raining. A little wind came up, the sea got choppier. Wave crests smashed the float, drenching them, and now he was shivering.

A rift suddenly appeared in the clouds; directly overhead was a pool of blackness, then the moon cut in to this dark pool, and he looked up at the full moon, brightening the clouds around it. Clouds racing across the moon made him feel better, then full of wonder that the night, the moon, and the sea could be moving along in the eternal rhythmical pattern as if nothing of any consequence was happening; when, in fact, they were there on the float.

"I suppose we might as well be sensible," Gina said suddenly, wiping her wet hair back. "Here we are, going somewhere. Why couldn't it be in the right direction? I've been seeing myself walking ashore. First there'll be a train — just a hop, skip, and jump from London. Then the Savoy. Rich and warm. The food brought to my room."

"I'll drop around and see you at the Savoy," Boseley said. "You can take me out to dinner."

"It's a deal," she said.

"I feel warmer already," he said. "Keep it up, lady."

"I used to like the way you all looked at me," she went on, her elegant tone sounding grotesque on the float.

"Aw, cut it out," Boseley blurted out. "Now you're making me feel cold."

"Then come over here close to us."

"Okay, Miss Bixby," he said. But as he tried to huddle closer the float began to tip, and he threw his weight hastily back where it had been. "My bloody luck," he said.

"Are there sharks around here?" she asked suddenly.

"Don't worry about sharks," he said.

"Sharks are afraid of dolphins," she said. "I read a long piece about dolphins. They're so friendly and beautiful, the piece said. The light of the world in dolphins. How about that?"

"Dolphins," Boseley snorted. "Oh boy, I'm in with a funny class of people."

"How do you know when your feet are freezing?" she asked.

"It's a fine warm feeling," Groome said. "You don't really feel anything."

"Then I'm not quite frozen," she said. "I'm really feeling it."

"Gina, come closer," he said. He knew Chone was watching, but he didn't care. He hunched closer and tried to put his good arm around her. Boseley, still a little afraid of him, watched them.

"That's a good idea," he said, and he too edged closer, trying to snuggle against her. But his move put all the weight on one side of the float, which took a sudden dip and water lapped in.

"All right, Boseley," he said sharply. "You know better than that. Don't tip this bloody float."

"So I stay here, eh?"

"You stay there. Keep moving your feet, Gina," he said.

"If my feet go, it's too bad — my feet were always one of my good points," she said.

"What's so good about them, Gina?"

"They're so small and that lets me wear sample shoes. I get good shoes at half the price. If I wait for a sale."

"Mr. Groome," Chone called with difficulty.

"Yes, Mr. Chone?" He had thought Chone was out of it, nursing his strength, maybe afraid of blacking out. Yet in the moonlight Chone had a determined big grin on his face. "You should marry a girl with sample-size feet, eh, Mr. Groome?" he said. In spite of his bad condition, Chone was still amused. The threat of his physical strength was gone; there could be no strength in him now but his silence. And having made his joke, he fell back on it now; and Ira Groome felt Chone there watching, and he felt the strange strength, too.

With the sea millpond-still, the float rocked them in a soothing, gentle little motion. The bright, hard moonlight made

153

it feel much colder. His wet clothes seemed to have frozen on him; yet when he touched his duffle coat, it wasn't even stiff. Leaning against him, Gina sighed with exhaustion, and dozed. The float's little rocking motion soothed them all. They were silent and resting. Soon Gina was asleep. Then he heard her begin to mutter; a broken inaudible sentence, and then, as the nightmare's intensity increased, snatches of words and little phrases became clearer. Mason and Boseley listened, too.

"Gina," Chone said. Chone, too, had to listen to the nightmarish whispering of her words.

"No, come back . . . stay . . . make it warm, all warm. It is. It's nice." A little pause, a mutter, and then, "Tall Troy's on fire." She mumbled, he couldn't make it out, then "beauty like a tightened bow — a tightened bow that is not natural in an age like this." Rossetti. Yeats. In her dream she was in college again. He wondered, and he said loudly, "Gina, Gina —" Stirring, she muttered, "No, my name — my real name. Yes, it's Tula." And Boseley shouted,

"Tula. Well, what do you know? Okay, if it's what she wants, from now on it's Tula. Hey, Chone — "

"Never mind, Chone, Boseley," he said. "Just shut up. Did you never have a nightmare? And after what she's been through — "

"I've got a great ear for such stuff, you know," Boseley said.

"I said shut up," he said.

Sullen and sour, Boseley answered, "I can dream too, sir. Tula, eh?"

Then suddenly, as if still in a nightmare, she sat up, staring around wildly, her face death-pale in the moonlight. "Where am I?" she cried. Then her eyes were on him, she moaned, "Oh my God, Ira Groome. You, thank God," and flung open her arms. They came around him. He knew that Chone, having raised himself, his eyes glittering, was watching; and he didn't care. If in this moment of sudden waking into the wet cold, after her wild dream, she could no longer go on pretending, no longer go on hiding from Chone the truth in her heart for the sake of getting her terrible satisfaction with him, it was not the time to care. He clasped her in his arms. She held on to him, trembling, and he forgot about Chone. He slipped his hand into her duffle coat while she held him so close, and he cupped her breast; it reminded him of all the warmth he had ever known. Her wet head came against his face, her mouth was on his as the float slid down into a gully and rose, and a cresting wave splashed them lightly.

"Ira Groome, Ira Groome," she said "Where are we?"

"What is this?" Boseley yelled, laughing crazily. "I know what's the matter with you, Mr. Groome. You're quitting. You don't care anymore, and you start feeling her up in this wet cold like an Eskimo. Right, Mr. Chone?"

Chone said nothing. It was the power of Chone's silence that brought him out of the moment's trance.

"Shut up, Boseley," he said.

"Well, I'm goddamned cold, too. Let me in on it, Mr. Groome."

"Shut up, Bo," Mason said.

"Don't try and shut me up, Mason. You're just the bloody tiffy in the sick bay."

"When we get ashore, Bo, one of the first things I'm going to do is punch you on the nose."

"Boseley," he cried. "I'll have you thrown in the brig."

"Right now, sir, I wouldn't mind being in the brig."

Then, above the sound of the splash of a big breaking wave he heard Chone:

"Hey, mister . . . hey, mister . . . "

Hunching his way along the float to the place where Chone lay with his head supported by the rim, he bent over him.

"What is it, Chone?" he asked grimly.

"Just this," Chone said. There was enough cold light for him to see the contemptuous grin on the bearded face. "Just remember this," Chone said, breathing with great difficulty. "No one wanted her more than I did. No one knew more about her than I did. No one looks up to her more than I did. No one loved her more than I did," and then he coughed and wiped his mouth. "You were nothing," he whispered contemptuously. "Just nothing. Get out of here."

"Okay, Chone," he said close to his ear. "I know all about you. I know all about your fantasies, too. Save your breath. So you can save yourself later."

As he turned away from him, Chone said, "No." He had grasped that she must have told him her story, told all about him, and he couldn't believe it. "No," he whispered desperately. "No."

But Boseley, who had moved closer to Gina, said, "Hey, Miss Bixby. Miss Bixby . . . "

"What?"

"It's okay, eh? When it's this damn cold, a guy says anything to keep himself warm. Okay?"

"Okay," she said, putting out her hand to Boseley in a ridiculously polite gesture. As Boseley took her hand she tried to smile graciously. Then the float tilted badly. They heard a splash. Facing the direction of the splash as she was, she screamed, "Jethroe . . . no . . . stop him." Mason, the nearest one to Chone, had tried to grab him as he rolled his body over the rim, and now he grabbed at him again, leaning far over the rim, reaching for him with such a lunge that they all lurched to that side.

"What the hell is this?" Boseley shouted. "Stay down." Chone's head appeared just once, about eight feet away, and then it vanished.

"The lifebelt. Where's his lifebelt?" he shouted.

"Jethroe," she cried. "Somebody — somebody — " Then, her back stiff, her head high, she screamed and waited angrily, "Jethroe, come back here . . . come back, you bastard." Raising herself and perfectly balanced, not even rocking the float, she dived into the water.

"My God!" he yelled, then remained frozen in wonder, while she went swimming after Chone. She had said she was a good swimmer.

Coming to himself, he yelled, "I'll get her," and swung his leg over the rim.

"No," Mason shouted and grabbed him hard by the shoulders. "No! No! Come on," he shouted. "You're weak as a kitten. You'll drown. The lifebelt will keep her afloat. We'll look around." And he held on to him. "Sorry, sir," he said.

Boseley, who had said nothing, paddled vigorously after her, but the float hardly moved.

"My God, Boseley," he kept saying. "My God, my God." He was still bewildered by his stunned moment of indecision. "I could have grabbed her. Oh, God, I could have grabbed her," he cried.

"No, you couldn't," Mason shouted. "Nor could I."

In the darkness they couldn't see farther than ten feet on the water. When the float slid down a wave there was just the sloping wall of water, and with the float circling around, they weren't sure of any direction. If only there had been moonlight or even starlight!

"They'll last out there ten minutes at most," Boseley said.

"No, she'll call out. We'll hear her. Listen, Boseley," he said desperately.

Mason was shouting, "Here! Here!" and it was a frighteningly desolate, lonely cry. Boseley took up the shout. They were crying against the wash of the sea and the darkness.

"Listen," he said suddenly. "I hear her. Don't you hear her? Over there. I hear her." They listened and shook their heads. When he kept turning and pointing, Mason finally said gently, "Take it easy, No.1."

With the float drifting around aimlessly, he lay back, and neither Boseley nor Mason, who now were subdued, spoke to him, nor did they speak to each other. The long silence made him feel colder and weaker from the loss of blood. His left arm was going numb right to the shoulder. Gradually the sea became calmer, the sky just a little lighter, and waves no longer tossed spray over the float. Finally Boseley said,

"Excuse me, No.1. Didn't you know she was Chone's girl?"

"She wasn't Chone's girl."

"Then I can't figure it out," Boseley said.

"Figure out what, Bo?" Mason asked.

"You heard her."

"Yeah, I heard her."

"Well, what do you think yourself?"

"I don't know what to think. I know that when you're hysterical you do crazy things," Mason said.

"Up to then was she hysterical?"

"No. But . . . "

"I could tell she was his girl," Boseley said. "I said so, didn't I? But his girl . . . that much? Not that much." After pondering, he said profoundly, "Hey, you know what she sounded like? A woman with three kids who catches her husband running out on her and shouts, 'No, you don't, you son of a bitch.' Right?"

"Well, come to think of it," Mason said, "the day we picked her up and I had her in the sick bay and she was coming to, she said strange things about him . . . Hell, I don't know," and he stared over the water. "I liked her a lot. She had a good style. How could that guy mean so much to her? I can't believe she was crazy. What about you, No.1?"

"Well, she sounded demented."

"Demented?"

"A demented jailer."

"I don't get it, sir."

"I don't either," he said bitterly, trying to believe no woman in love could utter that fierce angry cry, 'Come back, you bastard.' Then the vast, dark chilling loneliness of the sea gathering around him, while the numbness spread up his arm, made his opinion and his fate seem so unimportant that he wanted to hang on to the memory of the warmth that had suffused his whole being when his hand had been on her breast and she had clung to him. . . . Right under Chone's eyes she had clung to him, as if they both knew that in the end Chone couldn't count.

"Hell, what am I saying?" he said uneasily. "I just don't know." But this moment of sure secret knowledge — this is how he saw it — comforted him. "What's the matter with me, Mason?" he said suddenly. "I feel very dizzy."

"Maybe I should loosen that tourniquet for a few minutes," Mason said. "It may be the circulation. Come on." Taking the arm out of the duffle coat, he loosened the belt. The arm began to ache. As Mason tried to press against the torn vein in the arm, and let the other veins free, his own hand got covered with blood. . . . "Maybe this is all wrong," Mason said. "But my instinct tells me to do it." After about five minutes, he tightened the tourniquet again. "You've lost more blood," he said. "But it's the best I can do."

"Thanks, Mason," he said. "You're a great physician." Yet now he felt even colder. While the float rocked him into a welcome drowsiness, he thought of the morning coming, of the sun gradually rising high; the sun baking his skin, the hot sun drying his clothes, the sea and the float all in hot sunshine. He dozed.

Boseley's voice woke him. He heard "I wonder who it is?" and he opened his eyes. The sky had got lighter in patches, big heavier clouds were moving grandly across the lighter patches, and one of these great heavy clouds broke, and as the moon came out, throwing a silver streak over the float, he saw Boseley reaching over the side.

158

"It's Jackson," Boseley said. "I wonder what in hell happened to him?" "He wanted to get to Kenya," he said. "He would have done very well in Kenya. He was sure he knew how to handle the natives." And when they had pushed Jackson away from the float to drift on peacefully by himself, perhaps in the direction of Africa, he concentrated on Boseley and Mason, who, if they had been on shore a little while ago, might have come to blows; and he would have bet on Mason, who meant every word he said. The float dipped, then drifted into a path of shimmering moonlight. It was as bright as day, and he watched Mason and Boseley and liked them both very much. Two very important men. And how fortunate he was to have such good men there with him. He fell into a doze again. When he awoke, he heard Boseley talking about the taxi business.

"I don't know as I should go back into the cab business," he said. "Look, I was in a hotel in Halifax, and I heard this guy talking about plastics. A businessman. He said the big thing after the war was going to be plastics. Everything made out of plastic. The whole world. Millions in it, if you got in on the ground floor. Why couldn't I get into plastics?" In the cold brightness his voice sounded loud and friendly.

"Okay, Bo, so now you're in plastics."

"And soon I'm rich."

"And you'll be offering me a job, eh?" and then Mason changed the subject. "I was just thinking, Bo, you may have said a very true thing back there."

"Am I supposed to be surprised? What did I say?"

"About grabbing at little things, shore things, when you're scared stiff. Like this," and he tapped his chest. "A picture of my kid sister. Here under my sweater. It was there in my ditty box. How did I think that picture could help me?"

"I think I know why," Boseley said profoundly.

"Okay, why?"

"A guy does these crazy things without knowing why. Take me. I had this broad's compact in my ditty box. I used to take it out, smell it, and remember things. So when we get hit I look around to grab at something and what do I grab? This crazy compact."

"A cheap thing you could get in Woolworth's."

"I could get the broad in Woolworth's."

"Why did you grab it?"

"Anything to remind me of the safety of the shore, see? If a little thing like a compact has to be saved, it makes you think something as important as yourself has got to be grabbed by someone . . . "

"That's a lot of crap," he said harshly as if he knew they had really been talking about Gina throwing herself into his arms, and telling him she did it only because he was the one near her, the one who reminded her of safe things ashore. "You should have told that to Chone," he said. "See if he'd believe it. He certainly didn't. Or he'd be here now."

"It's okay, No.1," Mason said quietly.

"Sure, it's okay."

"Yeah, Chone knew he was through," Boseley said.

"That's what I mean."

"A man knows when he's through," Mason said. "That internal bleeding, and maybe terrible pain."

"Mason — that wouldn't have made Chone quit," he said. "Not Chone. He wouldn't have believed it. It wouldn't make him quit."

"But he did quit. So why did he? Do you know, sir?"

"Well, maybe I don't. No, maybe I don't."

"Well, there you are," Mason said, and again they were subdued and silent.

A paper box floated by, and some fifty feet away an empty lifebelt, and three pieces of wood, and the last stars were growing dim. In that strange light, he watched the margin of the sea widening; then, numb and half-frozen though he was, he tried to sit up and join with the others and search the water under the brightening sky.

With the sea widening under their eyes, Boseley suddenly screamed, "Look! Look! Jesus! Jesus!" He had made out a ship on the water. Tearing off his duffle coat, then linking the sleeves around the paddle, he hoisted it, and screamed and screamed. In a little while they were working the light on the rescue vessel flickering out a message to the boats. The rising sun brightened the water as Boseley kept on yelling.

"It's all right, Boseley," he said. "See. They're coming. It's all right."

When the boat came alongside there was some difficulty; it looked as if the float would tip. The seamen kept shouting encouragement. They lifted him into the boat, and now he was so weak he was giving the seamen a great deal of trouble. In the long, slow row back to the rescue packet, neither he, nor Mason, nor Boseley took their eyes off the float. According to someone in the boat, the rescue packet had been picking up survivors all night long; twenty of the corvette hands were safe. And finally there it was, the warm haven, a small, beautifully peaceful-looking ship, coming closer.

When they were alongside the packet, ropes were flung down, and a ladder dropped.

"How the hell are you ever going to get me up that ladder?" he mumbled. When they got him up the side, blankets were thrown around him, a hot drink put into his trembling hand. They had to hold the cup to his lips. Ghastly pale though he was from the blood loss, he tried to give them a courteous smile.

"Thank you very much," he whispered.

TWENTY

The big gangling square-faced doctor had a crew cut, huge hands, and a gentle touch, and he said, "Not dead yet, eh, sport? Just on the way to bleeding to death. Feels warmer now. Everything nice and warm, eh, sport? A splinter dug into your arm. An engine running out of fuel. Be thankful someone put that tourniquet on. Well, I've stitched you up. Here. Take a little brandy." Then he took a pencil from his pocket and, using it as a pointer, lectured on the arm. "Here's what I've done."

"How about Mason and Boseley, doctor?"

"Okay. A touch of frostbite in the feet. That's all."

"Great. They're wonderful."

A steward came with a tray, thick soup, a chop, hashed brown potatoes, bread, and an iron pill. "We'll get a lot of those iron pills into you to make up the blood," the doctor said. "This isn't a hospital ship. If we could give you a transfusion you'd be fine."

"When do I get up?"

"Sit up any time. If you were a woman you'd make blood more quickly. Being what you are, just a man, it's slower. So, take it easy."

"What happens if I try and walk now?"

"Weakness. Dizziness. You'll black out."

"Come on, doctor. I feel all right."

"You're as pale as a ghost."

"All right." He motioned to the doctor to come closer. "Who's the man in the bunk there?"

"A merchant seaman, terribly burned," the doctor said, lowering his voice.

"Should I try and talk to him?" The doctor shook his head.

"And this ship?"

"A packet out of Boston. We sweep around following a convoy. Eating like a horse, eh? Good."

"Who's your skipper?"

"J. Elton Howard. You can't miss him. He's about seven feet tall. Now, see if you can sleep on through the night, too. Well, see you," and he left.

Finishing the food he suddenly felt very sleepy, and he slept through the rest of the day and into the middle of the night, when rough weather tossing the packet broke his sleep and he heard a voice so very close it startled him. It came from the bunk where the heavily bandaged merchant seaman lay. The voice went on brokenly, "I waited at the turning on the path, lad, and you weren't there. Went on down the road a piece, and you weren't there," and then a long sigh. In the darkness he waited to hear the voice again. In that awful silence it was important to hear the sound of the voice. He was sure the man was dying. Believing he was listening intently, he fell into a light nervous sleep, then woke with a start. The wind was blowing hard. There was a moaning in the wind, and coming from the wake of the ship he was sure he heard a pleading tormented wail, "Ira . . . Ira Groome . . . Ira Groome . . . " Only half awake, he sat up, listening intently, and trembling. Pleading with him for what? Wherever she was, and being like she was, did she know he would be feeling he had been betrayed; betrayed by his own insights, by his discovery of fancied elations, by his recognition of those silent moments between them when they had seemed closer together than most people are in their whole lives? And would she plead that he should not feel betrayed? In the dark, leaning forward on his hunched-up knees, he still listened intently as if he imagined she was crying out to him for his understanding, or maybe even for the absolution of sympathetic compassion.

Yes, all he had to do was understand what had happened, he thought bitterly, then it could never disturb him again: it could be laid away like all other fully understood things. Finished. So then in the dark he could put it to himself this way: Gina hadn't been able to conceive of herself belonging to Jethroe Chone. Her fierce pride, her whole sense of herself, was violated by her passion for him, and so there was a secret torment in her, and she tried to believe she loved a man named Ira Groome. She tried very, very hard, even to the point of believing she wanted to see Chone killed, and she did not face what was in her heart until the last moment, when Chone tried to take himself away from her. There it was. There was the understanding. She could have it, if she needed it, the thing well understood by him. Rest in peace, Gina, with his blessed understanding. So, why should she be after him now? What had he left that she wanted? Was it this strange and terrible loneliness that made him want to weep?

In his rocking back and forth, he stopped suddenly, filled with bitter protest. Why had he let all this happen to him? Just a year ago at sea, he told himself, they could never have got him involved in their lives; he would have been correct and impersonal with them, his mind would have been on the ship, only on the ship. On this crossing he hadn't been himself. Not since his first brush with death on the previous crossing, not since the hospital days, had he been himself; and that old doctor, short-legged and wrinkled and full of silent mirth, had known it, for he had tried to tell the doctor about coming out of the long darkness that might have been his death, and how the people around him, the people there in the hospital too, people who had their own private lives, their own secret worlds, suddenly seemed to

164

him to have their own faces too. Their own faces! And how wonderful they seemed, and how much curiosity he had about them. It was as if in his childlike wonder, still moved as he was to be alive, he believed that even the jungle terror of deep personal involvements could be wonderful, could bring him more of the intoxication of life. The old doctor listened and smiled and said, "Sure, I understand. You got too close to the sun. That's all right. But if you get too close to people, you'll find they eat you up, and there won't be anything left of you. However, don't worry, my boy, you'll get over it."

"Yes, I'm a naval officer," he thought grimly, and he lay down and shut his ears to the moaning wind, and shut his heart to his wonder about Chone, and to the voices in his own heart, and thought instead about tomorrow and about being dressed and out on the deck. He concentrated on seeing himself in his lieutenant's uniform, and did it so grimly he fell sound asleep. He did not wake up till noon when two seamen came in, pulled a sheet over the dead merchant officer, and carried him out. Through the opening of the door he caught a glimpse of the deck. A wall of mist lay across the door; the cabin could have been hanging there in the mist. The packet was cut off from the life that is in a convoy. No whistles marked the positions, no noise of the rattle, no rush to the battle stations. Yet still there were the wireless signals. Never out of the reach of the authority of the beautiful signals.

His clothes were there for him, and he got dressed and stepped out on deck, feeling no dizziness. The mist was clearing rapidly. The sun's rays, cutting into the mist, gave everything a soft shine. Soon the mist would be gone. Going slowly along the deck, he passed four seamen whom he did not know, then further along, sprawled out on the deck, waiting for the sun, he saw hands from the corvette — ten of them. Mason, who saw him coming, stood up. "Great to see you, sir," he said.

"Mason . . ."

"Yes, sir . . ."

"Shake hands with me."

"You bet I will, sir," and they shook hands. "Thanks for putting that tourniquet on my arm, Mason," he said. "I'll always remember you," and he took a good look at him, standing there, with his arms folded in untroubled dignity. "Where's Boseley?" Ira asked.

165

"Along there, sir. Complaining of his feet but still talking big." Then he told about other hands from their corvette who were bound to be picked up soon. After the sinking he had seen them in the whaler with Horler, who had been shouting and cursing at them. Ira waited for Mason to mention Gina and Chone. He didn't. This silence about them, Ira thought, was as deliberate as if they had agreed that what had happened on the float was never to be mentioned. It made him feel uncomfortable and he left, going along the deck, and soon he was wondering why he himself hadn't mentioned Gina, and growing troubled he asked himself if it was because he suspected that in his night-long ruminations about Gina he hadn't got her right, and knew it, and knew that he would have to go on and on wondering about her, then wake up out of a dream and hear her calling, then lie awake, baffled by his need, this dream need, to hear her calling to him.

Lost in his troubled thoughts he had stopped, then someone passing spoke to him and he realized where he was. He was near the bridge. There was the sunlit bridge where the tall young bearded captain was talking to the middle-aged burly pilot — two figures calmly and securely rooted in their places, their right places, and he kept staring at them raptly, then suddenly he felt immense relief. His life was here at sea, he thought. A good life with a high purpose. How did he imagine he could afford to let his wonder, or fancied cries from Gina, go on troubling him. The captain there on the bridge had picked up his glasses; a seaman at the light was flashing a signal. Everything in controlled good order. A world of wonderful dedicated impersonal relationships. And why had he never comprehended the freedom in this world, the freedom from the shore stuff? The agony and bafflement that came ashore when people got too close to each other? Captain Mallard knew about this freedom. Mallard and his wife. Yes, there could be a good life here. A life of some good high purpose all laid out for him, and where there could be relief in forgetting the voices in his own heart.

In the emergency cubicle in the hospital where he lay dying, footsteps in the corridor approached the curtain then retreated as if preparing the way for the trusted specialist. Ira Groome was uncertain about where he was. Faint hospital sounds came to him, then sea sounds again, then a blur of images and sounds, which was very distracting because he knew he had to concentrate on the one picture of himself on that deck looking up at the bridge. He had been ordained to relive the whole thing till he got to that place and understood what he had done there. The feel of the old seaman Horler's hand on his helped him to hold on to the scene. He quickened a little in wonder — watching himself in that scene committing his high treason against himself, a man bent on overthrowing his own nature.

And with the scene as a background in his mind he watched himself with pained astonishment going down that road of rigid dedication and never turning back. Lieutenant-Commander; his ship sank two subs. Commander Groome. Ribbons Groome. And all the decorations. A man who soon believed that he knew how ruinous it was to get personally involved with people. Cawthra. He thought of Cawthra, a man who kept secret places in his life hidden from the general dedication. There were other old friends, who, when he saw their faces, or heard their voices, evoked voices in him he wanted to forget, so he had become as impersonal with Cawthra as with everyone else, as a good officer should, and so he had acquired the habit, the protective habit, and the habit had taken him over, and all the time under the mask of his medals was his withering heart. Pascal. In college he had read Pascal; if you don't believe in God, if you haven't got the faith, then act as if you have, perform all the rituals of faith, and you will come to believe. That was all wrong. You ended up believing in the habits that took over your heart.

And there he was, an impersonal man, so successfully at home in an impersonal world. Big in Madrid, big in Tokyo, bigger than ever in São Paulo. Then Julia's face floated in on him, over that faint background picture of himself on the deck looking up at the bridge. The young girl's face, the face of Julia coming to him after the war and bewildering him, making him feel everything about him was wrong for her. The anguish in the pretty young face, her voice saying now, "Why don't you touch me like you used to? Touch me like you used to, Ira, when I seemed to be something strange and wonderful in myself."

Then her voice from just five years ago, after she had made a drunken scene before his friends: "Yes, you're so kind and so fair, Ira. Why can't you say 'I love you'? Say it, damn you, say it." Then the hard, painful moment as he said awkwardly, "Of course, I love you." Weeping, she seemed to be begging him to weep with her for lost things while he, struggling and feeling smothered, finally said, "God damn this nonsense, Julia. You have responsibilities. Behave, do you hear? Behave." And then her voice yelling, just before she passed out, "You poor son of a bitch." Yet he was the Lord in São Paulo. And my son didn't know me — never knew me, he thought. Chris — Chris — that wasn't me.

Then he saw Chone's face, Chone right beside him now, grinning at him. Chone, who was dead now and never to be remembered, had all the passion. He tried to keep Chone's face in his mind so he could feel some of the terrible excess of his passion, the terrible beauty in the excess, because Chone knew the truth about himself in the power and intensity of his passion. The truth in the passion, as he should be able to see now. As Gina had known. He saw now that there could be no life, no love, no truth, without the passion that shattered all the rigid things.

Then suddenly, as the sea came washing over him, the deck wasn't there, the bridge wasn't there, he wasn't there, all washed away, and he was alone in his mind's darkness with the pain and the wonder from knowing that at the place on the deck that had so suddenly vanished he had started down a road on which he had turned his back on the perplexity and the mystery of people that made up the real adventure in life. And now he seemed to be floating away from his own body. He could no longer feel Horler's hand on his. He was aware of a chilling emptyness; he was utterly alone in a terrible void. Then why this sudden unexpected brightness? Was this the brightness that came with dying?

The brightness must have come through a suddenly opened door, and in came calliope music too, then marching band music with extemporaneous horns, and he saw a street brightly colored in soft pinks, yellows, and blues, blending in a warm tenderness of color, and down the street came a marching band, a motley crew, the men with saxophones and horns, all dancing as they played, and with them were monkeys and dancing bears and many clowns. Their faces came in on him, amusing, ridiculous, saintly, sober, innocent and criminal faces, all coming in on him, a wild crew; men from the high-wire acts, acrobats, clowns tumbling at him; jungle faces, presidential faces, generals, and pimps, marching gaily up to him — bringing their circus into his heart again.

Then the sea rose around him and he heard Gina's voice in the waters calling, softly calling, "Ira Groome. Ira Groome . . ." Her voice comforted him. And the waters too were comforting as they closed over him, for it was not now like it had been after the attack on the submarine when he had thought he was going down for the last time and cried within himself, "Who am I? What is my name?" Again close to the sun. Closer and closer to the sun. Just before the blackness closed down on him he smiled faintly, for he saw a sunlit clearing at the edge of a jungle and into that clearing came a white leopard to sit in the sun, and then he was dead.